GODDESSES

3

MUSES ON THE MOVE

CLEA HANTMAN

AVON BOOKS
An Imprint of HarperCollins*Publishers*

For information address
HarperCollins Children's Books, a division of
HarperCollins Publishers, 1350 Avenue of the Americas,
New York, NY 10019.

Produced by 17th Street Productions,
an Alloy, Inc. company
151 West 26th Street, New York, NY 10001

Library of Congress Catalog Card Number: 2001119222
ISBN 0-06-440804-3

First Avon edition, 2002

Visit us on the World Wide Web!
www.harperteen.com

PROLOGUE

When we last saw our heroines, Thalia had it something bad for Dylan from Denver (aka Apollo in disguise). But thanks to the Furies' trickery, Apollo headed back to Olympus, thinking Thalia would meet him there. Wrong. The only things waiting for Apollo on Olympus were disappointment and heartache.

After a rousingly successful turn in survival class Polly and Era, at least, seemed closer to fulfilling their challenges. And though Thalia was crushed over the disappearance of the mysterious Dylan from Denver, all three girls looked forward to returning to their real home, years and miles away in Olympus, someday soon.

Yet there were no signs from the heavens, no word from their daddy or his messenger, Hermes. Nada. Zilch. Nothing . . .

ONE

Monday, 4:00 P.M., front counter of the local café, the Grind

"A caffé latte for Polly, I'll have a single shot of espresso, and hey, Era, what do you want?"

"An extra-large mocha. With whipped cream. And sprinkles, those chocolate ones," she said.

I turned to the exasperated girl behind the counter and continued our order.

"And an extra-large mocha with whipped cream and sprinkles. Claire, Pocky, what do you want?"

"A chai soy latte for me," said Claire.

"I just wanna Coke, thanks, Thalia—oh, and a muffin, one of those giant muffins. And an oatmeal cookie, too, please," said Pocky.

I turned back to the girl and placed the rest of the order, meeting her dirty look with my own equally unpleasant scowl. Then I plopped down on the couch with my sisters, Claire, and Pocky to wait for our drinks. I was in a foul mood.

Why? Well, for one thing, Dylan from Denver had disappeared into thin air. One day we were friends, maybe even more than friends, and then poof! He was gone, out of my life. As if I haven't already had enough of the "poof, good-bye" stuff. As in, "Poof, good-bye, Olympus," "Poof, good-bye, Daddy and most of my sisters and everyone I've ever known," as in, "Poof, good-bye, Apollo."

Another thing getting my goat was that we hadn't heard from Daddy lately or from his messenger, Hermes. And we were all coming along splendidly in the challenges Daddy had given us, so we were expecting to get word any day—telling us our banishment was over and we could come back home to Olympus, back to Pegasus and ambrosia, cloud-soft beds, and our six other beautiful sisters, back to the fragrant gardens and the golden apple orchards and oh, everything.

Really and truly, we had learned our lesson—at least in my opinion. Polly was actually starting to mind her own business and stick by her convictions (as in, not letting me talk her into anything bad). Era was becoming a strong, independent young woman instead of a boy-crazy dreamer with no willpower. And I was . . . um . . . working on it. My selfishness, that is. So where was the reward? Not that I didn't like earth, but frankly, the days were starting to feel a little ho-hum. And I was missing the fam and friends back home big time. Especially Apollo, my long lost best friend . . . my other half.

"So, girls, what've you all got planned for the Thanksgiving holiday?" asked Claire. Her formerly purple hair was now dark and tipped in yellow, a color perfectly matched to her favorite eye shadow.

Before Polly or I had a chance to come up with an acceptable mortal answer to that question, Era chimed in, all curls and smiles. "What's Thanksgiving?"

"You're kidding—you guys don't know about Thanksgiving?" questioned Pocky, like we were three total freaks (albeit three very fashionably dressed and cute girl freaks).

I have to say, I was mortified. But then Claire jumped in. "Oh, silly me, of course you don't know about Thanksgiving since you girls are from Europe. It's a totally American holiday."

"Oh, right," I muttered, thankful for that we're-exchange-students-from-Europe story we told when we first arrived here in Athens, Georgia.

"Wait—holiday? Does that mean we get days off from school? Like how many?" asked Era, thrilled by the prospect of some time away from school.

"Yeah, we get a four-day weekend—everyone does," said Claire.

"I love Thanksgiving!" cried Era, her already rosy cheeks reddening even more with pleasure.

Suddenly I felt my bad mood drifting away. Four days away from homework. Four days away from the rumors that are always circulating about me and my sisters and how weird we are. Most important, four days away from the Furies. The Furies, who never let us forget they're here, that they're three strong complete *with* magic, that they're powerful and they're watching us, waiting for the slightest mistake to send them tattling to our evil, might I even say ugly, stepmother, Hera. "Four days without the Backroom Betties!" I said enthusiastically.

Our drinks arrived by way of yet another snooty-looking Grind employee. We all fell silent.

After the gal left, I broached the subject casually. "So, tell me more about this Thanksgiving thing. You Americans have so many cool holidays."

"Okay, so like back about four hundred years ago, way long ago, a bunch of people in funny hats came to America, well, to Plymouth Rock, supposedly, to escape religious persecution," said Claire, wrapping her hands around the chai soy latte. "So they got here and, well, the Indians were already here. They decided to join them in a dinner party to celebrate this new country."

"No, no, no, that's not what Thanksgiving is about," complained Pocky. Pocky was a little taller and a little thinner than everyone else at school. But he made it even more noticeable by wearing his orange hair in a mohawk as tall as it would go and his clothes as big and baggy as he could get away with without them falling around his ankles.

Pocky continued. "Thanksgiving is all about food and, okay, giving thanks for those good things in your life, but mostly it's about food. Like a big golden turkey and mashed potatoes and gravy and sweet potatoes with marshmallows and—"

"Leave it to you, Pocky, to see the holiday as a food fest," Claire interrupted disapprovingly.

"Yeah, well, this year I don't get any of that," he said, sulking. "My parents are going to Barbados and leaving me at home alone. They thought by throwing some cash my way, it would make it all better. But no, it doesn't. No sweet potatoes. No pie. No turkey." He was almost in tears.

"I wish my parents would throw some cash at me and be on their way," said Claire. "I requested that this year they perhaps try making something, I dunno, less cruel. I just can't sit at that dinner table while my brother and father tear at that poor defenseless turkey like it was their last meal on earth. But noooooo, Mom just laughed at me."

"Maybe we should celebrate Thanksgiving together, Claire," said my kindhearted older sister, who always agrees with Claire's feelings about animals. You know, if Polly had been born an animal instead of a goddess, I'd say she would've been a graceful swan because she's got all the beauty and gentleness of a long-necked bird.

"Or maybe we should take advantage of the four-day weekend and go somewhere we've never been!" I yelped. Brilliantly, I might add.

"Yes, yes! I want to go to the chocolate factory—where is that exactly?" asked Era of no one in particular.

"No, no," said sensible Polly, her eyes looking downward. I think she was trying to communicate to us that we should have this discussion later, when we were alone. But we ignored her.

"You guys should go on a trip. A road trip!" encouraged Claire.

"Yes, a road trip!" I cried, although I didn't know what that meant.

"Wait, you guys don't have a car—what was I thinking?" said Claire.

Oh, a road trip involved a car. A trip to anywhere involved a car. The thought brought back my bitter mood. The *Furies* had a car. Two, actually. A sleek little black one and this big contraption—something people call a minivan. It was an ugly, horrid shade of pink—at least that made me feel better. But still, Daddy could have at least given us a—

"I have a car," said Pocky, with all the enthusiasm of a Roman fairy* amped up on sugar pellets.

Now my sister Polly's eyes were huge and angry and raging blue. I could tell from her disapproving side glances that she didn't like this conversation in

---

* They're almost annoyingly perky but fun to hang out with if you're in the right mood.

the first place and now the thought that Pocky, a mortal, might join us for four whole days nonstop? I think that just made her livid.

"But wait, what about your host parents, guys?" asked Claire.

Polly sighed with relief and started to say, "That's right," but I interrupted her and said that our host parents (ahem, our *imaginary* host parents) hated holidays in general and would be happy to have the house to themselves for a weekend.

Era cried out, "Yes!" Her thin, long fingers danced in the air.

"I can't believe I haven't had a chance to meet them yet," Claire replied. "They sound so wacky."

Polly just sank lower and lower in the deep, furry brown couch, her porcelain features set into lines of frustration. She couldn't fight us, at least not in here, in the dark space of the Grind with all these people around. Plus it was two to one. Three to one if you counted Pocky.

"So when do we leave?" I blurted, continuing to ignore Polly and getting more and more excited.

"Well, we can leave right after school on Wednesday. It's a half day, so we're out by noon," said Pocky. "And I have to be back by Sunday afternoon to pick up my parents from the airport."

"Right. Okay, then, it's settled—we leave Wednesday." This was really happening. I felt a shiver run up my backbone. And Wednesday was only two days away. And on top of finally getting to go on a real earth adventure and spend a few days away from the Furies and have fun with my sisters and Pocky, there was something else. A teeny tiny possibility had been nibbling at my brain for the past few minutes, and now it was quickly turning into a plan.

"I wish I could go with you!" cried Claire, pulling me out of my secret plotting mode for a minute.

"I wish you could go, too, Claire!" I said.

"Well, I'll be thinking of you guys while I sit there in front of the poor dead stuffed bird."

"Oh, speaking of that," said Pocky, "I'll go anywhere you girls want to go since you're our foreign guests and all. My only request is that on Thanksgiving Day, I get some turkey—sorry, Claire. And mashed potatoes and gravy and stuffing and, let's see, cranberry sauce and pie . . ."

"Fair enough," I agreed, jerking my head up and down. "Anything you say, Pocky. Anything." Pocky, Claire, and Era gave me weird looks. Polly just closed her eyes and rubbed her forehead miserably.

But c'mon, how could I contain my enthusiasm? I was going to see America. I was going to get a bigger glimpse of what this earth thing was all about (somewhere else besides Athens, Georgia). And if I had my way, I was going to end up in Denver. That's right, the hometown of one cute, quirky, did I mention cute, football player, the one boy besides Apollo I had ever cared for: Dylan from Denver.

And that, my friend, would be worth all the pie in Georgia.

✳ ✳ ✳

Oh, dear Muses, can you be so naive?
We Furies would follow you beyond Tel Aviv.
Those are Hera's orders, for it was us three she chose
To torment you on earth—from your heads to your toes.
We heard you speak loosely and wildly of a trip
As we hid in a corner, nibbling cheddar cheese dip.
You've used your powers, and for that you will pay,
But in the meantime more fun's on the way.
We don't know how, but we'll come up with a scam
To turn your vacation into a shim and a sham.
Yes, we swear on our hairstyles and our mauve minivan
that we'll make a mockery of your Thanksgiving plan!

✳ ✳ ✳

Two

Back in Olympus, on the tippy top of Mount Samaras

Many miles and years away, Apollo waited for Zeus on the top of the flattest mountain in Olympus. They had a tennis game scheduled, but Zeus was a no-show.

Apollo wasn't in the mood for a game, anyway. He hadn't been in the mood for much of anything since Thalia had duped him into coming back to Olympus alone. All that begging Zeus for a chance to help the Muses, all that running around disguised as a football player from someplace called Denver, and for what? For Thalia to break his heart all over again.

He had stopped playing his lyre.* He had stopped going on adventures. He had stopped fighting crime. All of his favorite things.

In fact, the sun had not set in days and it was all

---

* A harplike thing that Apollo usually plays day and night. It really bothers many of his god neighbors.

Apollo's fault.* But Apollo had neither the will nor the energy to even *pet* his horses, let alone command them to gallop through the skies.

Even his own twin sister, Artemis,** couldn't rouse him for archery or a good game of golf. No, Apollo was down and out. Devastated. Depressed. Things were dire.

It was quite shocking, really, that he had in fact shown up for the scheduled tennis match. But he was curious. He wanted to see if Zeus had any news about Thalia. He couldn't stop caring. In fact, he really didn't want to.

When he realized Zeus wasn't coming, part of him longed to go back home to his own small castle in the clouds and bury his head in his silver satin sheets. But the bigger part of him had to know about Thalia. So he went to Zeus's very large castle in hopes of hearing something, anything, about his love.

A sprinkle of dust and he was in the castle's dark and cavernous waiting room. Most of the castle was bright and cheery, but Zeus had purposefully created this room to be as ugly and torturous as possible. He was the all-powerful and mighty Zeus, and he had a reputation to uphold.

Apollo looked around for servants, but none appeared. And then he realized why. That screaming.

* The sun was stubborn and stayed where it wanted to until the hunky and powerful Apollo rode his chariot by and demanded the sun set or rise.
** His loving virgin twin sis who spent her days getting out her frustrations by killing wild beasts.

That high, shrill, evil voice. It would scare anyone away. Anyone who wasn't determined to find out at least a nugget of information about the girl they loved.

Apollo crept up the stairs toward the noise. Eight doors down on the right he found the source. It was coming from Thalia's old bedroom.

He pressed his ear to the door (and he really didn't have to—when Hera screamed, all of Olympus heard).

"I don't care, Zeus, the girls have used their powers! They broke *my* rules. . . . They're done for!"

"Now, Hera, be reasonable. They've been getting very good grades in that mortal high school, right? Era even got a B in some survival class! And Thalia, her movie got an A-plus!" Zeus's voice sounded very desperate.

Apollo was delighted to hear that his film project with Thalia had scored her a perfect grade. That had to count for something.

"Grades?" Hera snorted. "I don't *really* care about grades. I didn't send them down there to get an education, I sent them there to punish them for being evil little children who don't know their place in society."

"But Hera, you were the one who made it a condition that they get good grades!"

"Oh, I don't care if they win the National Science Award. I just wanted to give them headaches. They're

rotten little scoundrels. They deserve to rot in Hades,*
and that's just where I intend to send them!"

"*No!* No, now, Hera, now be reasonable—you are
not sending my beautiful girls to Hades. I'm putting
my foot down, no."

"I don't care where you put your foot. I gave them
rules for their life on earth, and they broke them. The
Furies have reported that they have used their magic
freely!"

Apollo crumpled to the floor. Sitting there, so far
from Thalia and her sisters, he felt even more help-
less, if that were possible. Apollo continued to listen.

"No, they didn't use it freely, Hera, honey bunny,
they used it in bits, and my God, they went from living with magic daily to cold turkey, no magic! I love
you, my sweet, but what do you expect?"

"I expect respect. I expect grace and dignity, and I
expect that I don't have to worry about my own step-
daughters turning me green! I expect you to let me
handle this situation, and I expect you to continue
helping me with this harp—my music recital starts in
just three hours!"

"Look, dear, sweetums, I will give you respect, but
I will not let you send my girls to Hades. No, they
haven't been that bad, well, outside of that horrible
little Apollo debacle."

Apollo's ears went red as he thought of the horrible night that Thalia's sisters had helped her turn

---

* In essence the god hell. It's an ugly, dirty, abominable place, unfortunately ruled by the dastardly evil three, the Furies.

herself green to avoid marrying him . . . and accidentally turned Hera green in the process. His heart
burned so fiercely, his arms just dropped to his sides,
lifeless.

"Yes, well, I wasn't too keen, Zeus, about your
decision to send Apollo down there in disguise to
help them, but it all worked out in the end, now,
didn't it? Thalia proved herself to be simply wretched
yet again." And then she added, "Apollo got what he
deserved!" It stung his ears like a hundred and one
bees. He could hear the smile on Hera's face.

"Yes, my little chickadee, well, I was very disappointed in her for that, yes."

"Then let's get her and get her good. To Hades!"
And at that moment the hallway went black, and a
wicked wind whipped though the space where Apollo
was sitting, and he felt cold, wet, and chilly.

"NO!" Zeus bellowed.

And the wind stopped.

"Zeus, listen to me and listen well. I set the rules
for this game; therefore, I get to punish the girls
when they break them. It's out of your hands, it's
God's laws . . . but I tell you what. I'm so convinced
that they will break my rules again, that they will use
their magic freely and they will never fulfill your silly
challenges without it, that I'm willing to give them
one more chance before I send them to Hades. One
more. But I tell you, dear, as I stand before you, they

are going down. Straight down to the darkest depths of eternal damnation—they are going to Hades." And then her infamous cackle rang out through the whole castle, throughout all of Olympus, probably throughout all of Greece below.

Zeus was quiet. Apollo couldn't move. He knew he could be found out for listening in and would probably be punished severely, but he couldn't pick himself up. He pictured Thalia in Hades, cleaning up after the dreaded Furies, doing their laundry and their wicked deeds, and he slowly stood up, clenching his fists.

"I can't . . . I can't . . . I can't get involved," he said aloud to no one but himself. "Thalia's pushed me away for the very last time."

THREE

*Wednesday, 12:30 P.M., the front curb outside
the Muses' home, Athens, Georgia*

"We'll wait out here," Pocky said, revving the engine of his bright yellow convertible as Polly, Era, and I scrambled out of the car and into the house to get our bags. Finally! The half a day of school had been as torturous as a ferry ride through Hades. All I could think about all morning was getting on the road and getting to Denver, pronto.

Not that I had broached the Denver topic to my sisters yet. Believe me, I wanted to, but this was our first real trip on earth. Convincing them to spend it on finding some random boy I had shaky feelings for, even while having shaky feelings for Apollo to boot, wasn't going to be easy. It wasn't like I could blurt it out and expect them to go along. Especially since I was supposed to be on my best selfless behavior.

No, getting to Denver was going to take cleverness, panache, maybe even major flattery. But I wasn't worried. In fact, as I ran around the house, getting the last of my things together, I was thrilled. I was beyond ecstatic. I was . . . falling flat on my face. Era and I ended up on the living-room carpet in a heap of limbs and black plastic bags.

"Girls, get ahold of yourselves," Polly demanded, her own cheeks flushed in a mixture of anger and anticipation. "Okay," she said, softening. "Let's just calm down for a second and make sure we have everything we need."

Era and I nodded silently from our spot on the ground.

"Clothes? Check. Underwear? Check. Canned veggie cutlets? Check . . ." Polly continued on down the list, which she had pulled out of her skirt pocket.

We hadn't really known *what* to pack. In the past, when we wanted to go on a small trip, we just coerced Pegasus into sneaking away with a song or some fudgy-coated carrot sticks. If we needed anything along the way—a cleaner velvet robe, more delicious food, a harp—we just blinked it so. But that wasn't going to happen here, so we'd stayed up all night, packing everything we could think of.

Finally we finished going over our items, I yanked my favorite backpack onto my shoulders and snatched up a few bags, and Era and I started half running, half hobbling toward the front door (those bags were heavy). But before we got there, I felt a hand grab the back of my shirt. Era and I turned at the same instant to face a very solemn-looking Polly.

"I'm going to try to stop giving you these lectures, but before we go, I must say this." I let out a sigh of impatience, my left hand clasping the doorknob behind me. I hoped this wouldn't take too long. "Whether you believe it or not," Polly continued, "I'm just as excited about this trip as you are. I do have some reservations, but I think we're going to see amazing things and learn about places we never knew existed." *Not if we stand here all day gabbing,* I thought impatiently.

"But we are going to have to be extra careful not to reveal ourselves to Pocky. And please, *please,* let's remember why we're here. We need to grow up. That's what our challenges are all about. We need to change what's worst about ourselves. I think this is the perfect opportunity for us to focus on that. Era? Thalia? Can we please try?"

Then Polly gave me the most earnest, most thoughtful look and waited for my answer.

Sheesh. All I could do was nod.

"You brought your trash?" asked Pocky as we loaded our stuff into the back of his mom's car.

"No," I said, trying to think of a good solid mortal reason why we had our stuff in trash bags. What kind of bags were we *supposed* to pack? These were the biggest ones I could find.

"It's called packing, Pocky," said Era, saving the day with attitude. Pocky laughed.

"Okay, girls. You came all the way from Europe and you don't have, like, real suitcases?"

"Give 'em a break, Pocky," said Claire, who'd come along to see us off. "Like they're gonna drag huge heavy suitcases on a little weekend trip. I like their fine plastic luggage. It's *très* chic."

Man, I wished she was coming. Claire is like my mortal mentor. She teaches me all the cool words. She gives me all the good gossip. And she always lets it slide when I act like a freak from another planet. Polly just looked mortified.

"We brought snacks," said Era, holding up bags of gummi bears and chips and pretzels and more.

"Excellent! I knew traveling with you ladies was going to be divine."

"Oh, I wish I could come with you," said Claire. "So hey, where did you guys decide to go?"

We all stood there just looking at one another in an awkward moment of silence. This might be our one and only earth trip. None of us had been bold enough to take the lead. Not that I didn't want to.

Why, oh, why did Polly have to make that speech? Why couldn't my personal challenge be something besides being less selfish? Like learning to control my temper. Or learning to have more patience. Or learning to pay more attention. Really, I had more than enough bad traits to choose from.

Polly quietly asked Pocky if there was anyplace he wanted to go. After all, he was driving.

"Girls, I feel free. I love the road. As far as I'm concerned, I'll drive till I can't drive anymore. As long as I'm home in time to pick up my parents from the airport on Sunday, I am but your handsome driver. So, shall we go north? South? East or west?"

I'd looked on a map (a funky, modern version of the kinds of maps they have in ancient Greece), and I knew Denver was west, but now I felt guilty and suspicious even picking that *direction*. So I said nothing.

Polly rustled through her purse and pulled out her own map. I was impressed. "Well, I was thinking we could go someplace historical." She spread the map across the hood of the car. We all gathered around it.

"If you want historical, Polly, it's a trek, but we should really check out Colonial Williamsburg," suggested Pocky. "It will probably be awesome this time of year, too. Everyone dresses up in colonial clothes, and they reenact life in colonial times, like cooking and shopping and just about everything. It's all about re-creating the birth of the United States. And there are old gardens and even animals that they had in olden times. And they talk funny. It's a hoot."

"That sounds perfect, just perfect," cried Polly. I

didn't have half an idea of what he was talking about, but I felt queasy. What if that was nowhere near Denver?

I quickly scanned the map, looking for Colonial Williamsburg. I couldn't find it, and I panicked. "Where is it on the map?" I asked.

"It's in Virginia, just due north," explained Pocky.

I searched the map. Virginia was superclose to Georgia. But it was a whole map away from Denver.

"No!" I cried. "I mean, um, do we really want to sit around and watch people walk around in silly old clothes? Ptooey, that doesn't sound like much fun. It sounds boring."

"It's not bad, Thalia," said Claire. "I've been with my folks. It's kind of interesting, and the clothes are amazing." I looked at her with my best please-don't-help look.

"C'mon, more interesting, Pocky, name someplace else historical but more interesting," I pleaded, hoping he would psychically read "more interesting" as "closer to Denver."

"I think Colonial Williamsburg sounds great, Thalia. It's exactly what I had in mind," said Polly sternly.

"Hey, we're just looking for options. Now, Pocky, where else?"

"Um, okay, there's the Alamo. It's an old mission where just a handful of men defended Texas against the Mexican army for like thirteen days. The best part is you get to go inside and scream at the top of your lungs, 'Remember the Alamooooooo!'"

"Yes, but where is it?" I was growing impatient.

"In Texas, silly. San Antonio."

I scanned the map. Texas was huge! And not too far from Denver. I mean, it was only about an inch and a half!

"The Alamo sounds great. C'mon, Pol, what do you say?"

"Well, what else does the Alamo have besides a place to yell?" Polly asked unhappily.

"Uh, not much," said Pocky.

I was losing this battle.

He then said, "There's a cool gift shop that has stuff like sheriff badges and cowboy hats."

"C'mon, cowboy hats, Polly—you'd look great in a cowboy hat," I said.

I sounded pitiful.

"And," Pocky continued, "there's a Ripley's Believe It or Not wax museum across the street. It's kinda cool."

"Ohhh, Polly, you love museums!"

"Well, it's not like a real museumy-museum," said Pocky. "I mean, it's sort of a museum of freaks."

"But it's a museum, and she loves 'em, don't you?"

Polly sounded so hesitant. "Um, well, I guess, but Colonial Will—"

"Alamo! Alamo! Alamo!" I just started chanting it, trying to get her worked up.

"Well . . ." She was coming over to my side. I could feel it.

"Remember the Alamo!!!" I screamed.

"Remember the Alamo!!!" Pocky screamed.

Era sorta mumbled it. "Yeah, um, remember the Alamo?"

"Fine. Remember the Alamo," said Polly.

Mind you, the Alamo didn't sound like a great adventure. It seemed tame next to anything Apollo and I would've done. But at least it wasn't Colonial Williamsburg. Really, I was doing Polly and Era a favor by steering them toward the Alamo because Williamsburg did sound seriously boring. And the fact that the Alamo was closer to Denver—it was a bonus, not really selfish.

We hugged Claire good-bye, climbed in the car (I took the front seat, of course), and were off with a sputter and a vroom.

FOUR

Back in Olympus, Apollo's sister was so worried about her
heartbroken twin that she booked him a day at the
internationally renowned therapeutic day spa at the
Beautorium. Mineral baths, seaweed wraps, saunas and
massages, the works. After a refreshing but long day,
Apollo headed to his last appointment to get his hair
coiffed by the premier hairdresser to the gods, Aristophanes.

"**A**pollo, your mouth may not be talking, but your scalp is telling me you are a seriously stressed-out god. C'mon, relax, unload, tell me your troubles." Aristophanes was massaging Apollo's scalp so vigorously that Apollo's mouth opened involuntarily and quietly uttered the word he hadn't spoken in days. "Thalia."

"Don't tell me you're still upset over that little wedding fiasco? It's been months now. You are a god,

Apollo, and a handsome one at that. Most of my female clients, they would give up their powers to be with you. They tell me these things."

"That's very nice of you to say, Aristophanes, but there's more to the story than just the engagement party."

"Yes, I know all about Hera's turn as a green monster. Oh, she was so mad at those girls. It took me three rinses and two strong dye jobs to get that green hue out of her hair."

"There's more to the story than even that. But I don't want to talk about it—it just depresses me." And with that, Apollo sank lower and deeper into the gold lamé barber chair.

"Sit up, Apollo. Now, really, I think it will help you to discuss your woes with me. It seems to help most of my clients. They come in here and tell me their secrets all the time. And I never tell. I just absorb. Really, try me."

"No, I don't think so. But thank you."

"Suit yourself," sulked Aristophanes.

They sat in silence for a short while—Apollo slinking farther down in the chair, Aristophanes commanding him to sit straight without a word, just a short tug on his hair here and there.

"Okay, okay, okay," said Apollo, the silence getting to him. "I knew she had feelings for me, and I really loved her, so after Hera and Zeus banished her and her sisters to earth, I begged Zeus to allow me to go, too, to help out, but he said I could only go in disguise, and I agreed, but then it turned out they weren't just banished to earth but by accident to someplace totally foreign and halfway around the world, and get this, into the future, and so I went as this silly football player—it's a weird sport they have in the future where people chase a funny-shaped ball and bash into each other, like the raging wild satyrs from the Balkans, only in matching outfits—anyway, she liked me, or liked Dylan, which was my name there, and I thought she didn't know that he was me, but then the last time I saw her, she said she did know it was me and she kept trying to kiss me and she promised to marry me and she said she would meet me back here but she didn't come and I was tricked. Again."

"Oh, brother, you got troubles."

Apollo was still gasping for air when he said, "I don't feel any better."

"I should say not. That's a horrible story. Simply horrible. I always liked Thalia—she's a little precocious but not mean. That doesn't sound like her."

"I know, I know, that's what I said. I tried to tell Zeus that something was wrong, something was odd, but he wouldn't hear of it."

"Yeah, well, there is no telling that man anything."

Just then the salon filled up with lightning, but it was gone as quickly as it came.

"I don't know what to do now, Aristophanes, I just don't know what to do."

"What do you mean, do? You move on. You let it go. You wash her out of your hair. Here, I'll help. This nettle leaf shampoo is great for that."

"No, that's the thing—I don't want to. Or I can't. I don't know. I'm scared for her."

"Why scared? She's Zeus's daughter, and she'll be fine. You need to worry about yourself."

"No, you don't understand. I went to the castle day before yesterday. I heard yelling, so I followed it, and it was coming from Thalia's old room. It was Hera and Zeus, arguing. Hera wants to banish the girls to Hades now."

"No, not Hades—she wouldn't!" Aristophanes's voice was full of fear.

"Yes, yes, she would."

"No, Zeus will never allow it. I'm sure."

"He might not have a choice. Hera is the one who sets the rules. And now they've broken those rules. Or so the Furies say."

"Wait a minute, you didn't tell me the Blessed Ones were involved!" Now Aristophanes stopped cutting. He put down his scissors.

"You don't have to call them the Blessed Ones around me. They're the Furies, plain and evil. And they're on earth, too, in the same town, at the same school."

"No!"

"Yes, and they're watching the girls' every move. Apparently they reported to Hera their use of magic. And now Hera, Hera has the power to send them to Hades forever and eternity!"

"Oh, this is tragic. So sad. Oh." Aristophanes took a seat next to Apollo.

"Now do you see? I'm scared, and I don't know what to do. But she tricked me. How can I stick my neck out for her again? How?"

"Wait a second—she only confessed that she knew you were Dylan the last time you saw her?" Aristophanes stood up again and circled Apollo's chair.

"Yes."

"And she was very forward, very amorous, you say?"

"Yes."

Aristophanes spun the barber chair around to face him. "And she was never that way before?"

"No, never."

"Well, forgive me for being so bold, but are you sure it was Thalia?"

"It looked like her, it sounded like her—why wouldn't I think it was her? Where are you going with this?"

"I have heard many things in this chair. Many, many things. And I tell you, Apollo, I have heard more than one story of a Blessed One impersonating another for their own gain. When it's a god they're impersonating, it drains them of their powers for a time, but they can do it. Is it possible . . . is it possible you were being amorously attacked by a Blessed One and Thalia was none the wiser?"

"I don't know. It's possible. She sure wasn't herself. She was smacking her gum, and I never saw Thalia chew gum on earth."

"What's gum?"

"It's a horrible substance that makes one sound like a hungry cow. No, I never saw her chew gum until that day. And her breath, her breath was so sour. I've kissed Thalia's lips before—she has the sweetest breath that ever breathed."

"She could've had something foul to eat, no? I hear earth has some disgusting food."

"It wasn't a food sour—it was an inner-soul sour. Wait! It was *an inner-soul sour*! That's it—it had to have been a Fury. How did I not see this then?"

"I dunno."

"You're a genius, Aristophanes, a genius! Thank you so much!" And Apollo jumped out of the chair and kissed Aristophanes on the cheek. "I've got to go, I've got to go back to earth and save her. You're a genius!" And with that he ran out of the salon.

"Wait, Apollo, your hair—it's only half done! And my smock, you're taking my smock!"

But Apollo didn't hear. He was a god on a mission.

He flew to his own castle and let his most trusted servant know what he was going to do. It was going to take a lot out of him to get back to earth, to get back to the future. He needed to warn someone because he wasn't sure even if he got there that he'd be able to make it back.

Apollo gathered a few things and went out onto the bedroom balcony of his castle. Just as he was beginning his meditation to jump-start his most extreme powers, Zeus appeared in front of him in a puff of black smoke.

"Don't do it, Apollo." His voice was deeper and more serious than ever before.

"You can't stop me. I won't let you, Zeus. I'm scared for her. Hades? I just can't let it happen. I need to warn her."

Zeus was a little shocked that after everything she'd done, Apollo was still willing to risk it all to help his daughter. He questioned this devotion. "Why?"

"I love her, sir. It's really quite simple."

"Hera will never allow this."

"I don't care about Hera!"

"Yikes, don't say that so loud. She may hear you. You *must* care about her. She has Thalia's fate in her hands."

"I'm the only chance they've got. I can go down there and warn them that the Furies are just waiting for them to use their powers. I can warn them that the consequence is Hades."

"I can't allow it, not again. Hera will surely punish the girls if I allow you to go. She's given them one more chance, and that's it. Don't you understand?"

"You know what I understand? I understand we're wasting time."

"I'll have to punish you. I don't want to, Apollo, but I have to."

"Fine, punish me, but I'm going."

"So be it. When you land on earth, your powers, they will be gone."

"I don't care. Do what you have to do, but I'm leaving now." He threw himself into a cross-legged position and closed his eyes.

"Fine, leave, go. But you will have to go as Dylan once again. And this time you won't have your powers once you're there. That means you won't have the power to get back or to summon other gods to help you get back. I have no other choice."

Apollo chanted the only time travel spell he knew.

"Apollo," said Zeus, "one more thing." Apollo opened his eyes for just a moment and looked at Zeus. "Please, please don't let them use their powers."

Five

Wednesday, 1:10 P.M., Pocky's car on Highway 10

"I've got to pee," I said. "Can't we please stop?"

"No," said Pocky without so much as a thought. He turned the radio up louder.

"I want a mochaccino," whined Era. "I need one. C'mon, please, it's been forever since I got to move my legs."

"I have to admit, I am a bit restless," said Polly. "Maybe we could just make a small stop, Pocky, please."

"Oh my God, you girls are terrible! We've only been driving for twenty minutes! At this rate we'll be lucky if we make it to the Alabama border by nightfall!"

"I thought the Alamo was in Texas." I panicked.

"It is! And Texas is hours and hours away, especially when we stop for pee breaks and mochaccino breaks and leg stretch breaks every freaking half hour."

"Hours and hours?" I asked.

"Yes, hours and hours," he said.

"Pocky, we're adjusting to road trip life—just give us this one thing. We'll be good after that. Promise," said Polly.

"I thought you said you loved the road," Era added innocently.

"Yeah, exactly. The road, not the rest stops!" He was about as intimidating as a big, spiky-haired, cream-filled chocolate éclair. "But fine. I'll stop in Monroe—there's a café there. It's just two exits away."

"Thank you, Pocky!" we all cried out.

"Aw, shucks, sure." We sat in silence the rest of the way there. I took the map from Pocky's side and casually started to peruse it. I just had to figure out how long it would take to get to Denver from the Alamo. I had no idea this road trip thing meant hours and hours of boring driving. It doesn't take any time at all to get anywhere back home.

Right off the highway we spotted a coffee shop called the Coffee Nutty Net Café. Before Pocky had even stopped the car, our doors were open and we were fleeing for the coffee and bathrooms.

"Wait," cried Pocky, "no large lattes or megamochas—we've got to make it to Texas before Sunday!"

Polly and Era ordered at the counter, and I hit the bathroom. On my way out, I noticed a cluster of computers in a nook to my left. I slyly wandered over and sat down at the first free computer. The Grind has a computer, and I'd used the Internet there (with Claire's help). I felt very worldly and wise as I placed my hand on the mouse. At that moment a girl in an outrageous fuschia shirt and tight pants glided into the space next to me.

Even in Olympus it's rude to stare. So I quickly turned my attention back to the screen in front of me and typed in *Denver*. Up came a quick listing about Denver, Colorado, the historic sites, the places you could stay, the football. *Huh*, I thought, *maybe that football uniform wasn't that odd after all*. It was a Denver thing. Anyway, I found a map and typed in my "starting destination" as the Alamo and my "final destination" as Denver. 1,136 miles. That sounded like kind of a lot. Yikes.

I had the nagging feeling that someone was looking over my shoulder, but when I looked over at the girl sitting next to me, she was focusing intently on her own screen. I got up and casually headed for the table.

"You did have to go, didn't you? I'm sorry for making you wait, Thalia."

"What? Oh, yeah, yeah, bathroom, right. It's okay, Pocky."

Two strangers were sitting with my sisters and
Pocky. They were dressed as outrageously as the girl
I'd seen over at the computers, and they were whis-
pering something to Era.

"Here's your single espresso," offered Pocky. "No
doubles allowed."

"Thanks."

"Meet our new friends. They're in a band." Pocky
gestured to the two girls sitting across from him just as
the girl from the computer pulled up a seat behind me.

"Yeah," said the redheaded girl across the table.
"We thought you guys might be, too. We just
thought you looked like hipsters, but you know, road-
weary hipsters. Like maybe you had a punk band or
something."

"No, but maybe we should start a band—that
would be more fun than this trip has been," said Era.
She was just staring at the girl next to her. She was
wearing these great black pants that looked like
leather. And she had glitter everywhere.

"We've only been on the road for half an hour—
give me a break, Era," cried Pocky, a little exasperated
with the Muse sisters.

"Being in a band is pretty fun," said the dark-
haired girl sitting next to the redhead. "We've
traveled all over."

"Really? Like where? Is the Alamo a good place?"
asked Era.

"Uh, the Alamo kinda stinks," piped up the blonde behind me. "It's nothing but a big old dirty empty building and some tacky gift shops."

"Hey, it's not that bad," yelped Pocky. Way to go, Pocky.

"You want to head east. New York is cool. It doesn't get any cooler than the Big Apple. There's so much to do and see, and the shopping is fantastic," continued the blonde.

Wait, wait, wait. What was happening here?

"I want to go to New York!" cried Era.

New York, I thought. Upper-right side of map. Yikes. It's superfar from Denver. Super-duper far.

"I'm also fond of Miami," the blonde added. "The beaches are hot, and the dancing goes all night."

"I want to go to Miami!" cried Era.

Miami? I thought. I have an excellent memory. Inherited it from my mom. Miami was at the lowest point on the right side of the map—way down south. Very, very far from Denver. Unbelievably far.

"Mmm," Polly hummed dubiously. Neither of those two cities sounded like they were up her alley. I breathed a sigh of relief. But then she turned to the blonde, who seemed to be the leader, and said, "Do you know anything about Colonial Williamsburg?"

"We just came from there!" she replied. "We played a gig there, and it was a blast. I mean, the costumes are amazing—the girls know how to dress.

And the gardens are magnificent, you know, if you like that sort of thing."

"We like that sort of thing," cried Polly.

"And let me tell you," whispered the redhead to Era, "the boys there ain't so bad, either."

"We like that sort of thing," concurred Era.

"No!" I finally yelped.

"Yes, Thalia, yes," said Polly. "If these people think it's cool—wait, what's your band's name?"

"The Beautiful Omen."

"If the Beautiful Omen say it's cool, it's got to be cool. And I said I was going to stand up for what's right for me from now on, and I want to go to Colonial Williamsburg. Pocky, let's turn the car around and head for Virginia!"

Pocky threw up his hands. "Hey, you know what? Wherever you wanna go." And then in a funny accent he added, "Milady, your wish is my command."

"But—but . . ." This was unbelievable. We were turning around? Heading directly away from Denver? I tried to think of some good reason we should head west, but I was coming up dry.

"Why are you so intent on going to the Alamo, Thalia?" asked Polly, supersuspiciously.

"I'm not. Whatever—Colonial Williamsburg is fine."

I had to concede. I had to be selfless. Because I had no good reason for wanting to go to the Alamo other than the best reason, and the most selfish reason—Dylan from Denver. And I just couldn't tell my sisters that. "To Virginia it is."

✳ ✳ ✳

Denver, CO. Well, it's no surprise
That's what was revealed to Alek's spying eyes.
It's Dylan that Thalia is hoping to follow.
She still doesn't know that he's really Apollo.
Our plan is now clear and easy as pumpkin pie.
We'll keep the Muses away from Denver and spy.
The longer they stay, the more heartsick Thalia will be.
She'll resort to forbidden magic trickery.
Frustrated and desperate, she'll use her own powers
And be banished to Hades—to forever be ours.

✳ ✳ ✳

Six

Wednesday, 4:10 P.M., Pocky's car on Interstate 85

"I can't believe they're asleep—it's not even dinnertime," whispered Pocky. I had to admit, I was feeling a bit sleepy myself. This driving thing wasn't nearly as fun as it sounded.

"So are we there yet?" I asked quietly, so as to not wake my sisters.

"No, we're not there yet!" Pocky's voice grew louder.

"Well, it just seems like we've been on the road forever," I complained.

"We've only been driving two hours since we changed our minds and decided to head for Virginia."

"I didn't change my mind. I wanted to go to the Alamo."

"Why? Why were you so bent on hitting the Alamo?"

"Um, you just made it sound real fun, that's all." I was getting too good at this lying thing. I thought about confiding in Pocky about Dylan. He didn't know about my promise to be more selfless. But I just couldn't.

"Oh, well, Williamsburg will be real fun, too, I swear."

"Yeah, if we ever get there." I pouted and looked at the map for the eighteenth time in the last hour and a half, despite the fact that I now had every inch of it committed to memory.

Virginia didn't look that far on the map. But here we were, still in the car, and oh my goddess, that sign said we were just now crossing into South Carolina! That couldn't be! That meant we'd been in Georgia this whole time. We still had to go through South Carolina and North Carolina before we even entered Virginia. This was bad, very bad. At this rate I would never get to Denver. Not only were we heading in the opposite direction, we were doing it at a phlegmatic snail's pace!

I pulled out Dylan's note from my pocket, the one he wrote me before his parents took him out of school with no notice and moved back to Denver. It read,

> *Thalia,*
>   *You make me so mad sometimes. And so very happy. Most of all you make me laugh. I just*

*wanted to let you know how special you truly are
and how much this has meant to me.*

By the time you read this, I'll be home.

Till you are with me . . .

XO

I just had to get to Denver and talk to him. I had
unresolved feelings. For him and for Apollo, and
don't ask me why, but I was sure that talking to
Dylan was going to somehow automatically sort out
my feelings for Apollo. Not that I could do anything
about Apollo. He'd probably never speak to me
again. He probably hated my guts and innards and
intestines, too. And then there was that pesky little
he's-miles-and-centuries-away problem. Still, I missed
his smile and his recklessness and his ability to find
the best adventure and make time stand still. That
sure would come in handy about now!

Time stand still. Time stand still. Actually, I
couldn't quite do that. But truth be told, I *could* get us
to Williamsburg faster. Much faster. And if we got to
Williamsburg faster, we could see the sites there and
start heading to Denver.

But no magic. I promised Polly and Era, not to mention Hera and Daddy. Of course, we had used magic
for Polly when we were punishing that horrible Tim*

---

* A hairy high school boy, who may or may not have been controlled
by the Furies, who in book 1 used my sister for her artistic genius only
to humiliate her on open-mike night by stealing her song and discred-
iting her honor. We then stole his memory.

guy. And nothing bad came of it, no lightning filled the sky, no horrible, life-threatening messages from Hera, nothing. In fact, things had turned out rather well.

And if I got us to Williamsburg quicker, then Polly would be happy and get to feel like she chose the destination, and then I could get to go to Denver, too. Which really, if you thought about it, fulfilled my challenge in a way because I got to be more self-less (helping Polly) and still get what I wanted (Dylan). So using magic in this situation would really be a very, very good thing. In fact, I was almost positive that my sisters would have wanted me to, if they were awake.

I made sure we were on a generic stretch of high-way—trees, trees, and more trees. It had been like this for the past two hours, so hopefully it was like this the whole way. I closed my eyes tight and visualized us somewhere closer, much closer to Williamsburg. I wiggled my ears, twice on the left, thrice on the right, and intoned the name of Nike, the goddess of speed.

And suddenly everything shifted. We'd made the move. Not that you could really tell—there were still tons of trees everywhere and not much else. I looked over at Pocky, who was blinking and rubbing his eyes, as if he felt something was a little off but didn't know what. Then he just yawned and settled farther into his seat. I looked back at my sisters, still fast asleep. I closed my eyes in relief.

I was just drifting off when Pocky shook my arm, hard. "Thalia, we—are—in—Virginia! When we left that rest stop, we were in South Carolina! It's still daylight!"

"No, silly, the last time I looked, we were in North Carolina, not South."

"I'm sure we were in South Carolina. At least I think I'm sure."

"Really, we'd been in North Carolina for quite some time. We just crossed into Virginia, right? I've got the map right here—it makes perfect sense."

"By my calculations we weren't scheduled to get into Williamsburg until something like one in the morning."

"You know, Pocky, you rock at history, but math isn't your strong suit. Your calculations just must've been wrong."

"Yeah, must've been wrong. It's just—"

"Pocky, it's been a long trip, you've had to deal with the crazy Muse sisters, and it's probably taken its toll. Trust me, we're in Virginia, and that's exactly where we should be."

SEVEN

Wednesday, 4:40 P.M., Pocky's car in the
Colonial Williamsburg parking lot

"I just don't understand it, Thalia—we just got here way too fast."

"Trust me, Pocky, that trip wasn't all that fast. To me, it was treacherously slow. Hey, Era, Polly, wake up, we're here."

"Wha? Finally!" said Era, her curls all tousled and smooshed from falling asleep in the back of the car.

"Really, we're here?" asked Polly.

"We're here. You guys slept the whole way, practically."

We all climbed out of the car and stretched our legs. I couldn't believe all the cars everywhere. It was like the parking lot at the J-Mart, only a hundred times bigger.

"So what's first, Pocky, any suggestions?" asked

Polly, who was now not only awake but brimming with energy. We trailed Pocky out of the parking lot up to a ticket booth, where he said, "Four, please." Polly insisted on paying for the tickets, which were these little slips of paper we had to show to get into the town. Then we walked into what I could only assume was Colonial Williamsburg.

Right away I noticed the clothes. There were tons of women running around with long dresses and these weird little hats. The men all had ponytails with ribbons in them. It was kind of cool. People were riding in chariots much nicer than any I'd seen in ancient Greece, but still not nearly as nice or as shiny as the cars people drove now (and these ones were still being pulled by horses).

"Well, let's see, we could go tour the gardens while it's still daylight. Or we could get tickets for a show this evening."

"So wait, this is supposed to be America, like, a couple hundred years ago?" Era asked.

"Isn't it wonderful?" Polly said. "It helps to explain how things came to be the way they are today. That's what I love about history."

I shrugged, watching a pair of teenage boys, ponytails and all, walk by. They were gazing at Era, and when she looked up and noticed them, one of them actually blushed.

History shmistory. Besides the hair and the

clothes and the chariots, the people of Colonial Williamsburg seemed pretty much the same to me. All the more reason why we should just pop in, see the dumb gardens, check out a few old-fashioned exhibits, and skedaddle.

Just then three girls in full colonial garb crossed our path, nearly bumping into us. They stopped just a few feet away, leaning up against a fence. They looked very upset.

Pocky tried to continue. "Right on, Polly. Anyway, we could, um, go have an early colonial supper, or, uh, do those girls look like they need help?"

We all stared. The girls noticed our attention, and one of them gave us a shaky smile.

Pocky smoothed out his eyebrows and touched his hair. Yep, it was still standing straight up. Then we headed over to the fence.

"We noticed you over there. You look upset—can we be of any service?" said Pocky in his most well-behaved manner.

"Well, yes, actually we are in dire straits, young sir," said the shortest of the three, her hair in perfect blond pin curls. "We have the evening show to put on, and three of our primary young women have dropped out with a nasty bout of the influenza."

"Oh, bummer. I mean, what a shame, what a horrible shame," said Pocky.

"You know"—cough, cough—"Henrietta, don't

you think," said the tallest one, dressed all in forest green, "that these three girls would fit in the costumes just perfectly?"

"Oh, yes," squealed the one I could only suppose was named Henrietta. She had the rosiest cheeks and curls of red hair.

"Oh, no," I cried. "No, we couldn't possibly."

"Oh, but please," they all started whining.

"Of course we'll help you," said Polly, my sometimes annoyingly kind sister.

"Sure, can I wear a dress like yours?" Era asked Henrietta.

"Why, yes, indeed, it's quite like mine."

"What about me?" asked Pocky. "What will I do?"

"Oh, kind sir, we can use your help as well—you know we always depend on the kindness of strangers."

Pocky started to blush.

The taller one turned to me. "Please, milady, we entreat you to come to our aid in this time of trouble. We assure you of a rousing good time."

"How long will this take?" I asked.

"Don't be rude, Thalia," chastised Polly.

"I'm just saying, how long are we in for?"

"Oh, just a few hours of your precious time. Please?"

"Fine." What was I supposed to do? Scream, "No! I want to get the heck out of Dodge as fast as possible and make our way straight to Denver"? Oh, yeah, that would appear really selfless.

"Fantastic!" cried the girls.

"So what do we do?" asked Era, as excited as Polly.

"Well, you, dear girl, what is your name?"

"Oh, forgive us. I'm Polly, these are my sisters Era and Thalia, and this is our friend Pocky."

"Wonderful. Now, Polly, why don't you work in the foundry? It is a tad dirty work, a touch physical, but very rewarding."

"Um, okay, I guess." Polly didn't look as excited as before. I'm sure the thought of being inside a dark, dingy metal factory wasn't her idea of colonial fun.

"Era, why don't you try—" but she was interrupted by Polly.

"You know, I need to learn to speak up for myself, and, well, the foundry really isn't my cup of tea. Would there be anywhere else I could possibly go that might be better suited to my interests?"

"What about the printing press?"

"That sounds perfect! Yes, books, I would love that, thank you." Polly was perky once again.

"Era, now you, you shall go to the foundry in place of Polly."

"Oh, well, hmph." Era had now lost her enthusiasm. That is, until Henrietta leaned over and told her she'd be the only girl in a sea of cute foundry boys. Era was all aflutter in the blink of an eye.

"Pocky, dear sir, how would you like to try your

hand in the apothecary? I'm sure they could use an extra-strong arm over there."

"That sounds great—can I mix up potions?"

"Sure, just don't tell anyone." And the girls giggled together. Pocky just blushed again.

"And Thalia, since we know, or rather, we can tell that this isn't your idea of a good time, we saved the very best job for you. You'll work in the jail."

"The jail? The jail? And how is that fun, exactly?"

"Oh, trust us, it's one of the most popular places to work in all of Williamsburg."

"Sure. Fine. Whatever."

"Now head on over to that building and tell the woman at the front desk with the tightly wound bun that you are the replacement actors and you are in need of your costumes. We can't thank you enough, really, you are lifesavers, truly, and we are honored to have met you in such a fortuitous manner."

They bid us adieu, and my sisters practically danced to the front desk. I sulked behind. I tried to reimagine this as some sort of adventure, but I just couldn't take my mind off Dylan and getting to Denver.

Moments later we were each dressed in our uncomfortable and ill-fitting outfits. The girl who had previously worn mine must have been tiny since everything about the costume was short. Era's ensemble wasn't too flattering, either. She whined about her outfit being nothing like that of the cute curly-haired girl. But Polly and Pocky didn't seem to care. They each were in their own worlds, happy to be a part of this ridiculous extravaganza.

The woman with the bun pointed out where we should each go. We were spread out all over the park. The jail was housed in the farthest building of all. I walked there alone, thinking how odd it was that we hadn't even been in Colonial Williamsburg for five minutes when we were accosted and practically forced into acting ridiculous in front of strangers.

In fact, I had this nagging feeling that this whole situation was a little off. Whenever I have that feeling, I immediately think of the Furies. But I knew I was just being paranoid. Meg, Tizzie, and Alek were powerful, but they weren't psychic. They had no idea where we were. No, I was just feeling paranoid about my recent power usage. Plus I was in a bad mood. This colonial world was dirty, and frankly, it was missing all the best conveniences of modern life. No TVs, no sneakers, no phones.

Then I spotted one. An actual phone. Sure, it was disguised as some sort of colonial contraption, but it was indeed a phone. I looked around to make sure no one was looking. I pulled out the calling card Claire had given me and followed the directions on the back.

Ring. Ring. Ring.

"Hello?"

"Claire?"

"Thalia?"

"Yeeeee!" We both squealed in delight.

I just couldn't believe I could actually call Claire from anywhere. Anywhere!

"Thalia, where are you guys?"

"We're in Colonial Williamsburg."

"What? What happened to the Alamo?"

"Oh, Polly changed her mind."

"But wait, how are you in Williamsburg already? It should've taken you all night."

"Oh, that Pocky is a crazy driver."

"Uh-huh, really," said Claire, sounding more than a little confused.

"Anyway, you are not going to believe how horrible this is. Somehow we got roped into being in one of the shows, and now I'm dressed in this outfit that is two sizes too small on my way to do goddess knows what and I'm just miserable."

"You're actually in on the act? That's fabulous! Anyway, you got it better than me—at least you're out and about in the world. I'm stuck at home with my parents, who are on a crazy Thanksgiving crusade. They say they're going to force me to eat turkey, and they want me to wear a big Pilgrim hat."

"As we speak, I'm wearing a bizarre little thing called a bonnet that is so tight, I may just pass out."

"Relax, go with it. It's a fun place, Thalia."

"Fine. Sure. Whatever." I was looking for a little support.

"Oh, crud, here comes my mother. She's been looking for me, something about a reenactment of the Pilgrims' landing with my uncle Carl. I've got to go pretend I'm engrossed in homework. Gotta run, call again. Ciao."

And she hung up. There was nothing left for me to do but go directly to jail.

EIGHT

Wednesday, 4:40 P.M., Nova High, Athens, Georgia

Apollo landed on earth with a hard thud and immediately realized traveling in the future without powers was going to be harder than he had originally thought. How was he going to find Thalia? How was he going to get from one place to another? Then he reminded himself that Thalia needed him. He'd just have to figure it out.

Apollo felt something in his pocket. He pulled it out and recognized it as modern American money. He looked up to the skies for a second and silently thanked Zeus. He knew the guy had a heart.

Once again he was decked from head to toe in his football uniform. He had landed in the woods behind the football field of Nova High School. He crept onto the field and immediately noticed there was no one around. No one on any of the athletic fields. No one coming in or out of the school. He walked up to the side hall door slowly, only to find it locked. Apollo pressed his nose against the windows and looked in. The halls were oddly calm.

And then he saw a kid from Nova, someone he recognized from his and Thalia's media class, skate-board by. He called after the guy, but he didn't remember his name, so he just stood there, shouting, "Hey, kid, you, you media kid, stop." But to no avail. The boy just rolled on by and out of sight.

"Arrgggh," screamed Dylan. But no one heard. What was going on? Then it clicked. Of course. School was closed. He shifted direction and ran as quickly as he could to the Muses' house on Castalia Way.

He wasn't even out of breath when he ran up to the door in anticipation. He pounded and then gently knocked, fearing he might scare the girls with his mega-exuberance. But nothing. So he pounded again. Nothing. He ran around back and peered up into the huge oak tree where Polly liked to sit, but nothing. He pressed his face to their windows, but everything was dark. Nothing. He circled the house as fast as he could and then once again, slower, but nothing.

He feared the worst. He feared he was too late. The Furies had struck. Hera had succeeded. They were in Hades, and he was stuck on earth. It was the only explanation. But then after a moment or two of meditation to clear his mind, he realized they could be eating out or shopping or any number of mortal things they did on earth. He thought of hitting every one of their hangouts—there was no time to spare. Knowing Thalia, every minute was another minute they might be getting themselves into trouble. And then he thought of Claire. Yes, he'd try Claire's house and see if she was home first. And if she wasn't, surely her parents would know where she was. And perhaps she'd be with the girls.

He ran again, this time straight to Claire's, taking shortcuts through unknown backyards and an alley or two. He pounded on the door and then regretted it as he heard loud noises from inside. But at least there were people, live people, here. Maybe one of them would know where Thalia was.

A sour-faced woman answered the door. "Yes, what do you want?" she asked.

"Please, I must speak to Claire—is she here?" cried Apollo, out of breath.

"And who shall I say is asking?" She wasn't eager to get Claire.

"Dylan, Dylan from Denver."

The woman turned around and screamed at the top of her lungs, "Claaairre, there is someonnnne to see YOUU."

"Thanks, Aunt Sarah, who is—Dylan! Oh my God, what are you doing here?"

Thankfully it was Claire.

"Thalia, where's Thalia?" he managed to mutter.

"Nice to see you, too. What in heaven are you doing in town, D.? Are you here for Thanksgiving?"

"Yes." He nodded, although he had no clue what she was talking about. "So, Thalia, where is she? I have looked everywhere."

"You have, have you? Well, isn't that interesting—considering you seemed so eager to leave her without saying good-bye." Apollo wasn't sure what to say to that, so he didn't say anything. "Anyway," Claire continued, "you're out of luck. Thalia ain't in Athens. She and the girls went on a road trip with Pocky."

"With Pocky? Pocky? Why?"

"For some fun. They wanted to see the U.S. sights, I guess."

"But why Pocky?"

"What do you mean? Why not?"

"But she's not interested in Pocky, is she?"

"Well, you never know. That Pocky is quite the charmer, and after a few days on the road, and, well, where were you? Just some measly weird note and you're gone?"

Apollo swallowed the lump in his throat. Claire was just defending her friend. Did that mean Thalia had been sad when he'd left?

"Anyhow, she just called," Claire said, softening a little. "They're in Colonial Williamsburg. She was miserable because she had to be part of a show or something."

"What else?"

"That's all I know. I gave her a calling card and told her she had to check in with me often, you know, so I could live vicariously through them. I mean, I'm stuck here, and they're off having a grand ol' time."

"Yeah, okay, so that's all you know?"

"Yeah, Dylan. So why are you here? I can give her a message if you like. C'mon, tell me, why are you here?"

But Apollo didn't know what to say. He couldn't tell Claire to tell Thalia, "Don't use magic!" He just stood there looking nervous, trying to think quickly.

"Okay, um, well, I know they have to be back by Sunday," said Claire, "so Pocky can pick up his parents at the airport."

"That might be too late," cried Apollo.

"For what?" asked Claire.

But Apollo said nothing.

"I'll happily tell her you're in town, looking for her. You sure there isn't a message?"

"No." He shook his head. He *had* to find her before then. "Thanks. You've been a great help, thank you."

"You're welcome. Hey, have a great Thanksgiving."

"Uh, sure. Okay, thanks. Good-bye."

And Apollo walked away, defeated and crushed.

Did the Furies know the girls had left town? Had Thalia used any magic yet? Would Sunday be too late? And where was Colonial Williamsburg? All these questions ran circles around his mind, and he felt dizzy.

No, he couldn't wait, it couldn't wait. He had to get to Colonial Williamsburg and fast. But without powers, how? He needed a chariot. (He meant a car.)

He knocked on Claire's door again. This time, fortunately, her aunt Sarah didn't answer. Claire did.

"I need a car," he said rather abruptly.

"Excuse me?"

"How can I get a car?" he asked, like it was a perfectly normal question to ask in modern mortal times.

"Um, you can buy one. Or rent one, I suppose." Claire was looking at him terribly suspiciously, and he felt it.

"How much are they?"

"To rent? Your guess is as good as mine."

"What do I need to rent a car?"

"A credit card and a license, I guess."

"Huh," he said. "Claire, I need your help. Trust me, Thalia is in danger. I can't explain, but she is."

"This isn't some freaky jealousy thing over Pocky, is it?"

"No, this is serious. She is in trouble, and I need a car—I must help her."

"You look freaked, D. What's going on? Just tell me." Now she, too, looked frightened.

"She'd be in even more trouble if I did. Just trust me," he said, thinking of Hera's threats to punish the girls if any humans ever found out their true identities. "How can I get a car quick?"

"Well." Claire thought about it hard but quicklike. "Maybe, um . . ." She told Dylan to go hide behind the shed and that she'd meet him there in five.

A few minutes later Claire was handing Dylan the keys to her grandfather's 1987 Buick Le Sabre, which got driven about every once in a blue moon. "It ain't fancy, but it will get you there. Just please get it back as soon as you can, okay? My parents never go in the shed, but you never know."

"You're a lifesaver. Honest, I can't thank you enough, Claire."

"Yeah, yeah, well, you and Thalia have got a lot of explaining to do when you get back."

"I know, Claire, thank you again." And with that, Claire went back inside.

Apollo opened the car door and sat inside. But he had no idea what to do next.

NINE

Wednesday, 8 P.M., Colonial Williamsburg, Virginia

Finally this fiasco was coming to an end. My shift in the jail was over. I was going to grab the girls and Pocky and firmly suggest we hit the road. We could still make it to Denver tonight if—if—if . . . I used magic. Just a twinkle. Just a twitch. I felt bad, but c'mon.

NO! Wait! What were THEY doing here?

It was those ridiculously happy colonial girls who got us into this mess, and they were laughing it up with my sisters. I ran as fast as I could toward them.

"Hey, Thalia," said Polly. "So, was your day as great as mine?" she asked, beaming from ear to ear.

"Highly doubtful," I said. "I was in jail. As in, a prisoner. They said I was a 'witch' and threw me in the stockade. I got booed. One little kid threw his colonial mush at me while his parents rooted him on.

Now I just want to get out of these wretched clothes and get a move on. Where's Pocky?"

"Oh, you're gonna love the clothes we get next. They're not wretched at all—they're beautiful," cooed Era.

"What 'next clothes'? I want my jeans. I want my sneakers. I want to get the heck out of here."

"No, not yet," said the brunette colonial girl. What was her name? Oh, who cared. She was annoying. "The best part is yet to come," she continued. "We reenact the great Thanksgiving Ball."

"The what? No. No, no, no, no, no. We've got America to see. We've got country to cover. We can't possibly stay, but thanks so much, oh, so much for the offer. C'mon, girls."

"It's mandatory—all employees must attend," said the red-haired colonial girl. Jeez, she was more annoying than the other one.

"But we're not even real employees and—"

"We want to go, Thalia," said Polly firmly.

"You should see the clothes, beautiful ball gowns almost like the ones back home, er, I mean, the ones in the magazines back home. I mean, *those really old magazines.*" Era was grasping. Polly was shooting her the death look.

"I'm sure Pocky doesn't want to stay for a big ball. I mean, c'mon, this is the guy's Thanksgiving vacation. Where is he? Let's ask."

"Oh, he's still at the apothecary," explained the last colonial girl. "He was having fun mixing up his herbal potions. The head chemist has been showing him the ropes. He doesn't want to leave."

Okay, all three were truly annoying. Maybe it was something in the colonial water.

"We're staying, Thalia. Get over it—you're out-voted." Polly was in full confidence mode. She was sticking by her own desires instead of letting me bulldoze her into what I wanted. I was proud of her. Really proud. But her timing stunk.

"Fine. Where's my gown?"

Just then the red-haired colonial girl whipped out a truly stunning dress. It didn't look like the others, either—it was bright and vibrant and orange! It was awesome. It was going to look smashing on me. *Well,* I thought, *I'm miserable, but at least I'll look fantastic.* Dylan could wait an hour or three.

Moments later we were in the big hall with classical music blaring in the midst of a sea of fluffy ball gowns. The music wasn't quite as grand as the sweet sounds of the harps and lyres back home, and there certainly was less gold and glitter everywhere, but it wasn't bad. I joined my sisters on the dance floor and took a few twirls round and round with a boy or two. It was fun to let loose—it seemed like it had been too long.

But an hour later the fun had worn off. I guess I

had forgotten just how boring these sorts of soirees could be. There was nothing to do but dance. And you can't dance all night. Or rather, I can't. Era probably could.

Plus without Apollo around to make a little mischief—you know, slipping magic jumping beetles into the petticoats of stuffy old ladies and such—dances are generally downright dull. This was no exception. My sisters were off dancing with young colonial men, Pocky was nowhere to be found, and I was sitting in a corner by myself, wishing the evening would just go away. But I did have to admit, I looked good.

I thought about our day. What a day. I hadn't really had time to think in jail, with all the snotty little tourist kids taunting me. But now, with my sisters off and Pocky still gone, I couldn't help thinking about home. Not Olympus home. But Athens. What were the Furies doing? Had they noticed we weren't in town?

More boring music, more dancing. There wasn't even good food. I couldn't take it. My sisters had gotten over an hour of fun. Pocky had gotten yet another hour of potion mixing. Wasn't it my turn yet? I had to do something. I mean, we weren't even supposed to be here in the first place. It was all because those girls got sick and someone needed to fill their work shoes. This just wasn't fair. Fate had taken a left turn when it should have made a speedy right.

The girls. The sick girls. Surely these were their beautiful ball gowns. We were just replacements. If they came back, we'd have to give them their dresses back, right? And then we could be on our way. Sure, they were under the weather, but the best thing for that was getting out and putting mind over matter, right?

It seemed simple. It could work. Of course it would. It would just be a touch of magic. I'd blink them back here, to the ball, in search of their gorgeous gowns.

So I did it. I blinked. And then there they were, at the front door of the large wooden hall, dressed in normal clothes, their eyes scanning the crowd in confusion. I didn't hesitate. I grabbed Era out of the dancing arms of some foundry boy and with my other hand I nabbed Polly, who was chatting it up with an admittedly very handsome colonial guy. I pulled and pushed them toward the door and stopped in front of the three girls whom we had replaced.

"They're back, they need their dresses, we must return them, it's only fair, c'mon." I started unzipping Era's gown right there in the ballroom.

"No! I don't wanna give up this dress. No, I'm not leaving!"

"Era, it's their dress, not yours—you only borrowed it. Now let's go."

"No!" said Era. Polly just looked on, confused.

"I don't want to leave, either, but Thalia is right—these girls deserve their dresses back."

"Fine." Era was pouting.

Meanwhile the girls hadn't said a word. In fact, they looked a little, um, green.

"Okay, then," I said. "Let's go get Pocky and blow this cherry pop stand."

My sisters looked at me.

"It's an expression," I said.

We were almost out the door. So close.

"Thank . . . thank . . . thank." It was a meek, quiet voice. It was one of the girls. We turned to look at her squeak out the last word. But it never came. Instead a shower of vomit hurled from her lips. The crowd noticed immediately. How could they not? It was accompanied by a guttural shriek that resembled that of a horse giving birth to triplets.

It was all the girl next to her could take. She, too, looked a not-so-lovely shade of lime. She answered the first girl's vomit with vomit of her own. We gasped. I turned away for fear of vomiting in response. Which is exactly what three young women in the crowd did. Maybe it was the smell. It was enough to send me over, but I jumped outside for fresh air. I yelled for Polly, who stood there in the middle of the crisis, wanting to help but not knowing how. Era quickly came outside, too, totally grossed out.

I stuck in my head and argued with Polly. "We've got to get out of here."

"Thalia, these people need us, they need help. There must be twenty people vomiting! Look at this place—it's turning into a Vomitorium!"*

"Polly, if we get this heinous sickness, how will we get home in time for Pocky to pick up his parents? And how can we help? Magic? No!"

"Oh, but I feel horrible," cried Polly.

"I know, but I don't feel we have any other choice. We must leave—c'mon."

She slowly crept out of the hall.

"To Pocky!" I yelled.

We ran as fast as we could to the apothecary. Or rather, Era and I did. Polly sulked behind at a slow trot.

I threw open the door to the apothecary and screamed, "NO!"

The fates were not cutting me any breaks today. Pocky was there. But he was practically asleep. He looked a little ill, even.

"What's wrong with you, Pocky?" I demanded to know.

---

* This happened once before—the summer of 756 B.C. at the Oracle Hall. Dionysus had thrown the wildest party. Gods and mortals and monsters attended, and after a little too much sweet ambrosia Thaumas the Monstrous threw up. Well, that sight, a hideous creature throwing up mountains of white puffy crème, sent the entire party into a vomiting fit. The Oracle Hall was never used again, but from that day forward it was nicknamed the Vomitorium.

"It's this herbal potion the master chemist mixed up. It's made me very light-headed. Very woozy. Very silly. Hi, Polly, you're pretty. Hi, Era. Smile, Era. Hi, Thalia. Out of jail?" But he didn't wait for an answer. His head hit the counter with a violent thud.

"Well, I guess we are stuck here overnight, Thalia. He obviously can't drive," said Polly.

"We can't stay here overnight. I mean, we could get sick, influenza. We've got to get out of here."

"But how?" whined Era, who had plopped herself down in one of the uncomfortable wooden chairs in the apothecary waiting area.

"We can't drive. We'll have to use magic—we have no other choice."

"Of course we have another choice. To *not* use magic. Thalia, we can't. I suspect any day now we're going to feel the wrath of using our magic that time at the Grind. I don't think we can take another chance. No, I forbid it," said Polly.

"Look, we have to be back by Sunday. This is a modern mortal illness—who knows what it could do to us? And besides, it's only fair that we each get to choose a destination, and so far you're the only one who has gotten to make a choice."

"Yeah," Era added suddenly, jumping on my bandwagon. "What about me? There's lots of stuff I'd love to see. Like the chocolate factory." Now was my chance.

"Era's right. I think the only alternative here is to

use magic. Just a little. Besides, what harm has come to us thus far? The Furies aren't here—they don't have to know! The only reason we got here so fast is beca—"

"Wait, what does that mean? Have you used your powers?" Polly demanded.

"Well, sort of, um, yes. And see, nothing bad has happened to us."

They both yelled at me simultaneously so loud that I couldn't understand either one of them. Surprisingly, they didn't wake Pocky from the dead.

When they finally stopped to take a breath, I said, "Face it, Hera is probably not even paying attention to what we are doing down here. I mean, she's probably so consumed with redecorating our rooms, not to mention the sheer joy of having three less Muses around the castle, that she doesn't miss us at all. We're fine."

"She does get awful preoccupied with that decorating stuff," said Era.

"You know what? I don't care. Do what you want. *I'm not getting involved.* But I will not use magic," said Polly defiantly.

"Fine, we don't need your powers, anyway. Now help me carry Pocky to the car."

TEN

Wednesday, 11:29 P.M., parking lot of
Colonial Williamsburg, Virginia

"On to the chocolate factory," Era said as soon as we'd arrived at the car and leaned Pocky up against the passenger-side door.

"But Era, I don't think the chocolate factory exists." Era was still having trouble with the concept that lots of movies they showed on TV were make-believe. Or maybe she was just in denial about the chocolate factory. "Don't you wanna go somewhere else? Like maybe out west?" I suggested. I mean, I could've just point-blank said, "Era—pick Denver," but I didn't. It wasn't the time. We stood there, shivering in the parking lot.

"Hmmm, okay." Era looked thoughtful. "I pick . . . I pick . . . here in Colonial Williamsburg—let's just stay."

"Hear ye, hear ye, I agree. Now let's go help those poor people," said Polly.

"No, no, no, Era, you can't pick someplace we've already been—it's part of the rules," I said.

"What rules? I don't remember any rules," questioned Polly.

"Um, they're Pocky's Road Trip Rules, didn't he tell you?" Hey, how was it going to hurt him, blaming him while he was asleep?

"Oh," said Era sheepishly, looking at the sleeping Pocky. "Well, okay, but I dunno where." She furiously began twirling her blond curls.

"Blech, hurl, ptoot!"

"What was that?" asked Era, twirling faster.

"A bird, I think," I said, even though I didn't. "It sounds like a bird regurgitating food for its little infant birds. Now, where to, sis?"

"Blech, hurl, ptoot!"

"That isn't a bird, Thalia," explained my sister Polly, her normally pale face paling more. "That's some poor soul vomiting in the bushes. We should help!"

"How can you help? We may not be immune to a disease of the future. We can't risk getting sick—who knows how it may endanger us," and this last part I said in a whisper, "I mean, we're not exactly human."

"But . . ." Polly looked torn. She called out to the bushes, "Are you okay?" But nothing.

"What can you do for her, anyway? You can't make her better, you won't use magic. You're smart for sure, but face it, Pol, you're no doctor."

"Maybe she's right, Polly," said Era rationally, finally. "There isn't much we can do for these people. Maybe we should move on."

"Now we're talking. So, Era, how about heading out west, someplace like Kansas or Wyoming or . . . Colorado?"

"Well, I guess, I mean, where do you think, exactly?" said Era, looking way confused.

"Colora—"

"No! Don't let Thalia pick; it's not her turn," said my nosy sister Polly. "You pick a place you want to go, not one that Thalia wants you to pick."

"Now *who* is telling her where to go?" I said, and I could hear my voice—it sounded seriously snotty.

"I'm not telling her where to go! Era, I just want to remind you to make your own decisions. That's all, Thalia."

"You're not the boss of us, Polly."

"And you're not the boss, either, Thalia. I simply can't—"

"Enough!" Polly and I both fell silent. Amazingly, that angry, firm, booming voice was coming from my always sweet, always impressionable sister Era. "I know where I want to go. New York City. Now, let's go."

New York City? The only way we could get any

farther from Denver was to hit the ocean and start swimming. I opened my mouth to speak, but Era shushed me with a wave of her hand.

"There's this hotel. I saw it on *Access Entertainment* just the other day. Movie stars were staying there and going to this spa, which sounded a lot like the Beautorium back home. And they had water beds and huge golden swimming pools, and that's where I want to go, to the Hotel Royale . . . in New York City." And with that, she crossed her arms over her chest.

"Well, you know, they have, um, crime there, Era. Bad crime, haven't you seen *Cops*?" I said, grasping at straws.

"That's where I want to go, Thalia."

"But it's dirty!" I yelled.

"A Beautorium, Thalia, we need to get to a Beautorium. Look at my hair!" Now Era was screaming. It was no use.

"What's a Beautorium?" It was Pocky, leaning up against the car, groggy and half asleep. He was stirring.

"Oh, Pocky, good to see you're all right. Okay, we're off. Why don't you get in the car? Here, I'll help." I gave him a hand up and opened the backseat car door. He slid in and slumped back. I shut the door, and he slid down the window, stopping with his chin on the door lock. He started to drool.

I whispered, "Okay, okay, okay. Now that Pocky is up again, someone needs to drive till he falls back asleep so we can, you know, do our thing. I think that person should be me."

"Um, no," said Polly. "Why should it be you? You think you're better than us at everything earthly, but you're not. I think I should drive."

"Have you ever driven before?"

"No, have you?"

"No, but I watch very closely."

"Well, so do I!"

"Well, I think it takes some athletic prowess, and face it, I'm just more adept at these things than you."

"I don't think it takes athleticism; I think it takes a level head and smarts, two things you've proven tonight—and, dare I say, previous nights—you severely lack."

"W-well . . ." I stuttered.

"Plus I'm older, right, Era? Era, you choose."

"I don't wanna," she said, all quiet.

"That settles it," said Polly. "I will drive. Now get into the car. If we're going to go, let's go."

Polly got in the front seat, pulled on the seat belt, and clicked it into place. She put the key in the hole and turned it, and the car started right up. She looked so pleased with herself. For a moment. But then she panicked ever so slightly. She shook a little. And looked around furiously. She began to breathe heavily, and then she turned to me with an expression of extreme confusion and said, "How do you get it to go forward?"

ELEVEN

Apollo pulled into the Colonial Williamsburg parking lot with the same wild abandon that he drove those 528 miles from Athens. He stopped the car randomly, covering no less than three actual parking spots, and jumped out of the car before it had even stopped chugging. He was a man on a mission, a man with a one-track mind, a man who'd left the keys in the car. But that didn't matter. All that mattered was that he was finally within reach of Thalia, he was finally going to tell her the whole story—how he was actually Apollo in disguise, how Hera intended to send them to Hades if they messed up just one more time, how he still loved her after all the vomit and greenness and snakes. He loved her.

He ran for the nearest building, a small structure
with a sign out front that said Tickets. But he quickly
realized that the lights were out. He could see no one
inside. He hadn't thought about the fact that it was
late, after hours, and that most people were probably
already at home, asleep. He pounded on the glass of
the little kiosk—not to get anyone's attention, but
just out of sheer frustration. Now where to? He
scanned the parking lot and saw cars but no people.
He let out a groan, a groan of anger and pain.

"Can I help you?"

A little mousy face peeked out from inside the
kiosk. She looked like she had been sleeping.

"Oh, my, someone is in there! Thank you! I'm
sorry to disturb you, but can you please tell me where
I can find a young girl by the name of Thalia?"

"Don't know anyone by that name, sir, sorry."
She looked at him with a mixture of curiosity and
sleepiness.

"No, of course you wouldn't. I've missed them,
surely," he said. Apollo hung his head low, unsure of
what to do next.

"You know," said the woman from the booth,
"there's a big dance in the ballroom across the way. If
your friend is anywhere in the park, she would be
there. You go through those gates, take a left at the
silver shop, your third right after the magic store, and
then your fourth left after the bathrooms that look

like a public hanging spot. There's a big hall over there, and that's where the party is."

"Well, it is a dance, and Era and Polly love those things—they could be there. Yes, thank you very much! That's wonderful news! You can go back into your house and resume sleeping now."

"Wait!" She detained him a moment to collect money for a ticket. Then she gave him an awkward, confused wave as he hurried off into the darkness.

Apollo ran across the lot, through the gates, and made his first left, third right, and fourth left after the bathrooms that looked like a public hanging spot. Had he time, he would have liked to look around this village—there were candles burning everywhere, and beautiful gardens lined the walkways—it was lovely. He would have loved to be strolling here with Thalia right now, arm in arm. But maybe that wasn't such a far-off possibility after all.

Finally he arrived at what seemed to be the hall. It was a tall and graceful building, aglow with lights, but right away Apollo sensed that something was amiss. There was no music. No happy sounds. Just a few grunts and moans. And then he saw the crowd of people standing—or rather, crouching, kneeling, and sitting—on the front lawn.

Apollo hurried over to a man dressed in a very fancy suit, holding a hat in his hands and leaning against a wall. There was no time to ask any questions but the most important one. "Excuse me, sir? I'm looking for three friends of mine, and I was wondering—"

But before he could finish his sentence, the man opened his mouth to speak . . . and promptly vomited into his hat! Apollo watched in shock as the man ran off toward the woods, only to be sick again.

Apollo looked around for someone else to ask. But there was no one. Or rather, there were plenty of people, but no one to ask. Because everyone, every single person, was in fancy dress and violently ill.

"Thalia's been here," Apollo said to no one in particular. A place filled with unhappy, miserably sick people? He would have bet even the Keres* that Thalia had something to do with this mess. And the possibility that it might have to do with magic made him feel a bit ill himself.

After searching every face on the lawn and in the surrounding area, Apollo walked back out to the parking lot and looked around. He figured he could try all the nearby inns or perhaps the local eateries. But before he made it to his car, he spotted a girl in the parking lot coming out from behind a clump of bushes. She looked ill, but currently she wasn't vomiting. It was worth a try.

"Excuse me, excuse me, miss, can I ask you a question?" As he got closer, he realized she was clutching her stomach and still quite sick. "Uh, are you okay?"

---

* Winged chick demons pretty much responsible for all disease and death.

"I don't know—I feel weak, but I finally stopped throwing up. Who are you? A doctor?"

"No, sorry, not a doctor." Apollo had to turn away a bit—her breath wasn't sweet. In fact, it was rather vomity. "I'm actually looking for three girls, sisters. They're traveling with a tall, scrawny-looking boy with big spiky hair named Pocky. Have you seen them?"

"I don't . . ." She coughed. And wheezed. Apollo patted her on the shoulder.

"Never mind," he said, backing away. "I can see that it's a bad time and—"

"Wait," she said weakly. "I did see some girls talking, and they were with a boy, I think, with a mohawk. But I was out of it, you know, throwing up behind these bushes. I barely remember."

"Yes, that must be them. They weren't sick, were they?"

"No, I don't think so. They sounded like they were arguing."

"It's them, I'm sure of it. Okay, where did they go? Which direction?"

"I dunno. I'm sick."

"Right, um, think hard—did you hear them mention anything? Anything at all?"

"I think one of them asked if I was okay. I heard something about a bird."

She crouched and sat on the ground, then whispered, "Oh, they were talking about that show *Access*

Entertainment and some hotel with a spa or something. They were kind of yelling." She began to cough uncontrollably. Apollo knelt down, turned his head from hers, and shook her gently. He held her shoulders but couldn't face her. "Please, it's imperative I find them."

"Wait! I remember! It was the Hotel Royale. New York City."

Apollo let go of her shoulders, and she fell over. "Oh, sorry." He jumped up. "I've gotta run. I'm really sorry. I hope you feel better."

"Yeah, um, sure," the girl muttered from the ground.

Apollo ran to the car, turned the keys, which were already in the ignition, and revved the engine loudly. He still didn't have this driving thing quite down yet. He spotted an old box of Tic Tacs on the floor of Claire's grandpa's Buick. They looked like pills of some sort.

"Hey," he called to the girl who had helped him, the girl who was still crouched on the ground in pain. "Here." And he threw the box of mints her way, accidentally hitting her on the forehead. He felt really bad, but this was Thalia's life on the line. He had to go. *Now.*

Screeeech! Apollo peeled out of the parking lot and didn't look back.

TWELVE

We didn't waste any time. As soon as Pocky was asleep, I blinked our way to New York City. Unfortunately, Pocky woke up right quick and sat up straight with a jump.

"What? Where are we?"

"We're driving, see? Yawn. I'm sooo sick of driving," I said, even though we'd only been driving for a few minutes.

"This looks like New York City. What? Did I sleep the whole drive?"

"Why, yes, yes, you did," I said matter-of-factly, maybe too matter-of-factly.

"But then why isn't it light out? It should be morning. Didn't we leave Williamsburg late at night?"

"Yes, yes, we did," said Polly. She wasn't helping.

But who could blame her? She was busy trying to drive the car, dodging left and right. She looked panicked, but I have to say, she was doing a good job.

"See, Pocky, you've been sleeping for like twenty-four hours. It's not Wednesday night—it's actually Thursday night." How else to describe our five-minute jaunt to New York City? I had thought about telling him Era was in fact an expert mechanic who rigged his car to go two hundred miles per hour, but I thought the Thursday night thing was more believable.

"It's Thursday? No way! I must have been so out of it. What happened at that apothecary?"

"You drank something that didn't agree with you, apparently," I said. My sisters kept their mouths shut. Lying wasn't their forte.

"Wow, that must've been some drink."

"Sure was," I said, like I knew.

"So wait, that means it's Thanksgiving. . . . Did I miss it? What time is it? I can still have my dinner, right? We've got to get turkey!" His enthusiasm made us all a bit uncomfortable. I really didn't like lying to Pocky, but what choice did we have? "Where shall we go? Did you girls already pick a place?"

"No, we haven't." Polly's voice sounded so sad. She hid her beautiful face behind the wall of her straight hair in shame.

But Era didn't sound sad at all. "How about Greenwich Village? I have seen so much great stuff about that place on the TV. I bet they'll have a yummy turkey dinner!"

Polly and I both turned to her and gave her the "duh" stare. Did Era really think it was Thursday?

While Polly clumsily drove us toward Greenwich Village (I held the map), I hoped that Thanksgiving was like one of those holidays they celebrate all week long. We needed a turkey dinner with all the fixin's tonight. Then we needed to check into that hotel Era was so excited about, get some shut-eye, and hightail it to Denver tomorrow morning.

It seemed like that was never going to happen at this rate. Every thirty seconds Polly's foot slammed on the brake. We were moving even slower than when Pocky drove.

"St. Marks Place. Did you find it on the map? That's where we should go," said Era, all of a sudden an expert on New York City.

"Where did you hear of this place?" I asked.

"It's a street, a famous street. C'mon, did you find it?"

"Yes, I think we're close." Then we all fell silent because Pocky, Era, and I were just amazed by what we saw. Even though it was late, there were people everywhere, people like I'd never seen before—riding bikes, walking their dogs; people with hair even crazier and spikier than Pocky's; people singing and playing instruments on the streets. The buildings were enormous—they reached up into the sky. And the lights! They were electric lights, and there were more of them than I could have ever imagined. And the smells! Some of them were wonderful—like the most heavenly spices in the world were being cooked in these little stalls on the sidewalks—and some were terrible, like rotting garbage and goddess knows what else. But who cared? This was as divine a place as I'd ever seen.

We found a parking spot on MacDougal Street and jumped out of the car before Polly could even get Pocky's cruiser into the spot. It took her eight tries.

I looked around. There were three restaurants right next door to one another. Someone had to have turkey, right?

We started walking toward the row of restaurants. "You know, Pocky, it's superlate, and people might be out of turkey dinners by now," I said, hoping that this might explain why on Wednesday evening we weren't able to get a traditional Thursday night Thanksgiving dinner.

"Really, you think so? I'm sure someone will have some left."

A bunch of kids about our age walked by, and they all had different-color hair like a pack of those Life Savers Era loves to devour. A man stood on a street corner, blowing bubbles at traffic—he was very talented. We saw a group of women who just had to be Amazonian, they were so tall. There was a man in a gold lamé dress (or a very unattractive bearded lady), and he was holding these three crazy colored snakes.

We tried all three restaurants and even a fourth around the corner. None had turkey and gravy or cranberry sauce or sweet potatoes with marshmallows. Each gave us a look that all but said, "Tomorrow, stupid."

"Let's try St. Marks Place," said Era. "We can grab something to eat and a cup of coffee. New York coffee is supposed to be strong. I saw that somewhere. TV, I think."

"I can't believe I missed Thanksgiving dinner," said Pocky, who looked truly sad. I felt horrible. His only wish this whole trip was to have that turkey dinner, and now he thought he wasn't going to get it, thanks to me. And if he did manage to get it tomorrow, how was I going to explain that?

Era grabbed Pocky by the arm and started pulling him toward St. Marks. "C'mon, Pock, this is going to be fun. We'll get you some food, some yummy, sweet food."

Polly and I walked slower behind the two of them. "You can't keep this up, Thalia. The lying, the magic, it's going to come back and hurt you, hurt us all. I'm sure of it. Something bad is going to happen."

"I know, I know, I don't feel good about lying to

Pocky, but I don't know how to stop now." I had to admit, my plans had gotten a little out of control. But I was going to try to be better from now on. Really, no more magic. Not unless it was absolutely, positively necessary.

Inside the coffee shop was even wilder than out on the street. We actually spotted a satyr*! Or at least that's what I think he was. He had little horns on the top of his head just like the satyrs back home, and he had these markings on his face, like ink, just like them. I wanted to go pet him and maybe see if he knew my cousin Dion, but Pocky stopped me and said that he might be dangerous.

We got some food and some coffee (yes, it was strong!) and found a table toward the back. The coffee shop was dusty and dark and smelled of old fruit and burning wood. Two girls sat behind us, whispering and sipping these creamy, delicious-looking drinks out of big, cloudy glasses. We were surprised to see an old fortune-teller was setting up her table next to us. We all noticed her rainbow dress and turban, even amidst all the color. Apparently modern-day fortune-tellers hadn't changed all that much since ancient times.

Era used to love going to the soothsayers back home, and she couldn't resist now. She shyly asked the woman if she could read her future for her. The ancient woman agreed, "For five dollars."

* Half men, half goats who mostly hang out with my wild and crazy cousin Dionysus.

"You girls must have the biggest allowances of all time," Pocky said, eyeing the huge wad of bills Era pulled out of her purse. We hadn't made much of an effort to hide the fact from Pocky or Claire that we had an unlimited supply of cash. We'd always chalked it up to having rich parents back in Europe.

The soothsayer asked Era to sit down and then grabbed her hand and ran her fingers over Era's palm. She closed her eyes and whispered a few non-sensical words, then opened them with a pop. We all listened intently to hear what she was saying.

"You, my girl, are from a very far-off land. You are a lover of all things sweet . . . and beautiful. Hum. You will have a very boring life. Hum. Now, that is all I see—leave my table. Send over that girl who was sitting next to you." She nodded toward me.

Era got up, appearing very disappointed. That was worth five dollars? Even with an unlimited supply of money, it seemed like a rip-off. She'd been right about Era's personality, but her future-seeing skills seemed to be lacking. Yet Polly still seemed compelled to go to the woman's table and ask to see her future, too.

The woman sighed with impatience and glanced at me, as if for some reason she was only interested in reading my palm and not Polly's. She pulled out a small crystal ball and ran her hands over the globe furiously.

"You, my dear, have a very romantic nature. You are also gentle, and you love animals. I see that you have an antelope you like to ride. . . . No . . . wait . . . it looks like a horse with a horn on its forehead, which doesn't make any sense, but oh, well. I foresee that you will eat lunch tomorrow. Next? Send over the brunette."

Polly also headed back to the table, somehow looking both impressed and disappointed.

"That woman may be chintzy with the future info, but she's sure on target about you, Pol," I pointed out.

Era gave me a shove. "Thalia, she said for you to go over. We went—you have to go."

"But why? I mean . . ." But Era just kept pushing me out of my seat. "Fine, fine," I said. I'm not against a good fortune-telling now and then, but this woman seemed like a fraud to me. Still, I got up and headed over to her table.

As I approached, a strange smile crept across the woman's face. I handed her my five. She didn't take it. She just nodded for me to sit, and she pulled out her tarot cards. She shuffled quickly. All the time the smile stayed on her face. She only glanced up at me once. As she laid the cards out on the table, I noticed that she had the hands of a young woman more my age, but her face was wrinkled and craggy. It creeped me out. Her breath was awful stinky, too.

"You, dear girl, have a young, very handsome, I might add, man waiting for you on the top of a snowy mountain. Hum. He yearns for you, and his heart is breaking at this very moment, wondering where you are. Hum. His heart's fate is in your hands. Do whatever is in your powers, er, rather, power to get to him at once. Hum. That is all—now leave. Send the boy."

How could she know? I'd thought this witchy woman was a fake, but she had to be real if she knew about Dylan and Colorado. I sat in the chair for another moment, trying to comprehend what all this meant. It was obvious enough, I guess. I had to get to Denver and quick, for Dylan's "heart's fate" was in my hands.

"I said leave," croaked the old woman. I got up, also dazed, from her chair and went back to our table.

"She wants to talk to you now, Pocky."

"I dunno. She's kind of freaking me out. You girls look a little wack now, if you ask me."

"It's your turn. We all went—c'mon," said Era. "Maybe she can tell you where to get turkey and marshmallows. Ask her."

Pocky slowly got up and went to her table. He quietly sat down and pulled the wood chair up a bit. He wouldn't even look at the fortune-teller, he was so nervous. The old woman took a slow sip of her tea and then slammed her cup down on the saucer. She waved a single finger over the cup and then, as she peered inside, her eyes went wild with fire. She was reading Pocky's tea leaves—an ancient, ancient art.

"You, young man, have a wonderful future ahead of you, magnificent!"

Pocky finally relaxed, sat back in the chair, looked back toward us, and smiled.

"But there is a small hitch!" Her voice was sharp and loud and almost hurt the inside of my head. "You have a hex upon you, a very dangerous hex, and it must be vanquished before you may receive all the wondrous good that is awaiting you. Hum." She pushed the cup aside and pulled a business card out of her bosom. She handed it to Pocky and said, "My sister, the lovely Madame La Rue, specializes in hex removal. Hum. You see her at once. She is in New Orleans, on Old Chartres Street. It is imperative you do this immediately, boy. Hum."

Then loudly she said, "Now be gone!"

Pocky, gripping the card with all his might, stood from the table and walked toward us. "Well, that wasn't so bad," he said in a squeaky voice. "But, um, how soon do you think we can be in New Orleans?"

"But what about New York?" whined Era.

"And what about my turn to pick?" I cried, before I realized how selfish and stupid that would sound.

We were all silent for a few minutes. Pocky's face

was so white, his freckles looked bright orange. He cleared his throat. "I really wanted to see New York, too. And I want you to have a chance to pick, Thalia. But we're talking about a hex." He handed me the business card. "Please, Thalia, take this. And don't lose it. I have nowhere to put it." All those pockets and none of them actually opened. Silly pants.

"I'll put it in my backpack for safekeeping."

"New York or no New York, we have to get to New Orleans to remove that hex," Polly soothed. It was obvious that she believed every word the fortune-teller had said. We all did.

Suddenly Pocky's face lit up. "Now, wait, if we chill out here tonight, then leave first thing tomorrow morning, which is Friday morning, we could be in New Orleans by Saturday morning—well, if I drove through the whole day and part of the night. We could visit Madame La Rue as soon as we got there, and then, since New Orleans is at least in the south and somewhat near home, Thalia could pick one more place, of course, provided it's on the way, but it's totally doable."

We all sat there for a moment totally still because, of course, we knew it wasn't Thursday at all but Wednesday night. Yes, Pocky's plan was even more doable than he thought, but no matter what, my plans weren't. Not unless I used magic. I thought about the fortune-teller's words, "everything in my power." I had to see Dylan—his heart depended on it.

I spoke up. "I don't think—"

But Polly interrupted me. "Of course, Pocky. We'll do whatever we need to do. We owe it to you. I am sure we all agree that your plan will be just fine. Let's get to the hotel, and then tomorrow it's off to New Orleans to get this nasty hex removed. All in favor, say aye!"

"But . . ." I said. It didn't matter. I was drowned out by the loud chorus of ayes.

Colonial clothing, tarot, and tea leaves,
The Muses and Pocky are so clearly naive
To think that mere mortals can predict things to come.
Now I, Alek, head Fury, have them under my thumb.
I suspect all that gibberish threw their heads in a whirl
And will take them on a detour that will ruin these girls.
They'll keep using magic, and they'll find out real soon
The more magic they use, the more surely they're doomed!

✳ ✳ ✳

THIRTEEN

Wednesday night/Thursday morning,
12:36 A.M., Hotel Royale, New York City

"**It's** just like *Lifestyles of the Rich and Famous*!" screamed Pocky as we entered the room.

The inside of our hotel suite at the Hotel Royale was indeed amazing. It was the closest thing I'd seen to our castle back home yet. The curtains were thick and velvety. There was gold glittering everywhere. The beds were big and thick and luxurious. And the room was huge—there was plenty of space to waltz four couples wide, if we wanted.

Suddenly we weren't tired anymore. We read the hotel guide, and it gave phone numbers for things like "room service" and "health spa." Pocky couldn't believe we'd never heard of that stuff before, but he explained it all to us, anyway. And then we just went crazy.

We started by calling the fancy restaurant downstairs and begging them to make a midnight turkey dinner for our friend Pocky. With all the fixin's! And they said, "Yes, madam." Just like that. We spied on all the New York neighbors with the telescope that was set up next to our windows, which gave us a view of all these amazing buildings that were oh, so high. We turned up the stereo as loud as it would go and danced on the giant beds. Then Era said she was dying for a Roman massage, so we called up the desk and they sent up masseuses for us, just like that! They weren't skilled in the Roman massage, but we got something called "shiatsu" that was divine and maybe even better than at the Beautorium back home. After our massages the food came, delivered by men in tuxedos. Pocky got his turkey dinner with cranberries and sweet potatoes with marshmallows and mashed potatoes and gravy, and Era got the biggest plate of french fries I'd ever seen, and it came under a silver domed plate just like back home. Polly got a vegetarian feast of roasted vegetables and portobello mushrooms with currants and arugula and frisée and all sorts of things I'd never heard of. And I ordered the giant shrimp cocktail and lobster, and it came with its own bib. We ordered up two movies on the TV and sat back in bed, eating ourselves silly. We only made it through one of the movies before we were tossed into a serious food coma and sleep was upon us.

When we woke up the next morning, we pocketed all the fun little bottles of stuff in the bathroom, like shampoo and conditioner and those plastic hats that go on your head when you don't want to get your hair wet. We waited at the front desk as the desk guy swiped our credit card and gave us one of those receipt things (which I promptly threw in the trash). Then we headed out the door to hit the road and drive, unfortunately, south.

FOURTEEN

Thursday, 8:16 A.M., New York City

I knew something was different the moment we stepped outside. The streets were crazy busy. There seemed to be at least five times as many people out here today as there were yesterday. People were crowded everywhere, and there were tons of folks selling things on tables and blankets. It was kinda like being in Sparta for the Cretan bull run. There were people smooshed against one another as far as the eye could see. And it was hard to stay together with all the pushing and shoving. I could see Pocky in front of us, leading the way—no doubt with thoughts of Madame La Rue in his head—but all of a sudden Polly and I realized we had lost Era.

We backtracked a few steps and saw her kneeling on the ground, looking at a very dirty man's very shiny jewelry. She had loads of it on already and was looking closely at two more necklaces. Polly looked at me pointedly with her feet firmly planted on the ground. "No," she said. "I am making a choice. I will not be my sister's baby-sitter for the rest of my life. Go get her!" she yelled at me.

I ran back and grabbed Era, who dropped the jewelry she had in her hand but continued to clutch the items she had on. "Keep up, please, we don't need to lose you. There is no time." But Era wouldn't budge—she just kept looking at herself in the hand mirror. I set my backpack down and wrangled the baubles off her pale white neck.

"And what exactly is the rush?" she asked cluelessly.

"Hello? The hex, New Orleans, Denver," I said, without even thinking.

"Denver?" asked my sister. But I just ignored her question and grabbed her arm, and we ran and ran until we met up with Polly, who was just steps behind Pocky.

"Oh, wow, look at those enormous animals!" screamed Era.

"There's that dog from TV!" I cried.

"Look at the giant yellow bird!" squealed Polly.

We didn't know what we had walked in upon, but whatever it was, it was amazing. The crowds around us watched and cheered as these giant animals and cartoon characters floated up into the sky above us and continued in a long line down the street. We just stopped and stared. How did they get them so big and flying without a bit of magic? Pocky came running back toward us, frantic and out of breath. "Today, those balloons—it's the Thanksgiving Day Parade, so it must be Thanksgiving!"

We three looked at one another. I was sure that Polly and Era's guilty expressions mirrored my own.

"Uh-oh," I said.

"Um, huh?" said Era.

"Grgglee . . ." choked Polly.

And then I did it. I didn't really think, I just did it.

I blinked all the balloons away. Into thin air. Gone. Bye-bye.

"What balloons? What parade?" I said as guilt-free as I could muster.

Pocky spun around, peering up into the sky.

"But, wha—? They were here. They were . . . just a second ago. . . . I don't . . . You saw them, didn't you? Polly, didn't you? They were just here."

Polly just looked around painfully.

"Era, didn't you see them, the really big Snoopy? C'mon!"

"Um, no, I don't think so," she said sheepishly.

"But . . . but . . . the balloons, gone . . ." As Pocky stood there, confused, a loud commotion went up all around us. The people on the streets started yelling and running and pushing. I guess a lot of people besides Pocky had realized the cartoons and animals were gone. Oh, what had I done?

"C'mon, this place is turning into a wild boar race. Let's get out of here," I said as I tried to get everyone moving toward the car and fast. Polly shot me a look that said I deserved to be trampled by a crazed Roman horned pig and then started walking. But Pocky just stood there with his mouth gaping open. "It's the hex—my hex is causing me to go crazy. The hex . . ."

Polly and Era hurried ahead while I gently took Pocky's arm and told him we should get on the road, get on our way to New Orleans, on our way to Madame La Rue. With the mention of New Orleans he nearly tore off my arm in his rush toward the car. I followed a few steps behind. A vague notion nagged at the back of my brain—that things were spinning so incredibly out of control that I wasn't sure I'd ever be able to set it all right again. Ever. Then the thought was gone as I ran full speed to the car.

FIFTEEN

Thursday, 8:32 A.M., New York City

Apollo actually made it all 387 miles from Virginia to New York City in seven hours and twenty-one minutes. It wasn't a record. But it was pretty good for someone who'd only learned to drive the day before.

Unlike Era, Apollo had never seen anything about modern New York City on the television, nor had he read about it in books. To him it was just another place on a map, another place his wandering love had gone.

So while he noticed the crowds and the hoopla and the mayhem, he didn't know that this wasn't what New York was all about. Sure, it was crazier than anything else he'd seen in the modern world, but Apollo was a world traveler. He'd seen great races and horrible wars. This was crazy, for sure, but he'd seen far worse. And right now he had but one thing on his mind. He stopped many people, asking for the Hotel Royale, but most just seemed to be muttering cluelessly. Or pushing. Or yelling.

He finally found a policeman to ask for directions. While he stood there, patiently waiting his turn to talk to the officer, he listened to the other people's crazed questions.

"Where did they go?"

"Did you see them, the balloons? They were here just moments ago and then poof!"

"I've never seen anything like it! It was like they just magically disappeared into thin air!"

"Have aliens invaded the earth and taken our Thanksgiving parade?"

The questions hit him like punches in the stomach. No, this wasn't New York as usual. This was New York in chaos. And he was pretty sure that it wasn't the work of aliens, whatever they were, but of his dear Thalia. That it was the work of a magical Muse. A misguided magical Muse.

He felt sick. He thought he might pass out with worry. It was Hades for sure for the girls—they had obviously used their powers!

Apollo boldly yelled out, "Where is the Hotel Royale?" and maybe because this was a question the policeman could actually answer, unlike all the others, he turned to Apollo and told him, very slowly and carefully, how to get to the tall brick luxury hotel that was just a few blocks away.

Apollo scanned the crowd with every step he took. They had to be here somewhere. From the car, to the policeman, through the crowds, all the way to the Hotel Royale, Apollo looked at every face in search of Thalia.

He entered the hotel and went straight to the giant mahogany front desk, the one with the magnificent chandelier above.

"I'm looking for the Muses, I mean, Muse sisters. Are they here?"

"Is that *M-o-o-s-e*?" the man with the dull, fake British accent asked.

"No, *M-u-s-e*. They were here at this hotel—are they still?"

"One moment, sir." The man typed very slowly. "No, it appears the Muse party has departed. Couldn't have been more than an hour ago. You know, those girls really ransacked—"

But Apollo didn't wait to hear what the girls had done this time. If there was no more than an hour between him and them, he had a shot at finding them before they took off to not-even-Zeus-knew where.

He ran out onto the street into the swarming crowd. The scene outside had gotten worse. He could barely even see faces now, everyone was so packed together.

Apollo then heard a small cry, an old man's "Help!" from under the crowd. He looked down and saw a very old gray man, with a few pieces of jewelry clutched in his hands. He was getting trampled. Apollo bent down and helped the man to his feet, grabbed his blanket, a backpack, and his remaining jewels, and pulled him to the side, slightly out of harm's way.

The old man thanked Apollo. "What a day this has been, young man. First this girl, an amazingly beautiful girl, runs off with some of my best things, and she didn't even pay for them. Then the balloons, just *poof*, and then this craziness. It's like people think the world is coming to an end!"

"Here you go," Apollo said, handing the man the blanket and backpack he'd picked up.

"Don't know whose that is," said the man, nodding at the backpack.

It was green with little orange bits at the ends of the zippers. And a patch that said Girls Kick Butt sewn on the pocket. It looked familiar. Apollo glanced around quickly to see if anyone else was looking for it.

No one claimed the bag. Everyone was too busy pushing and shoving. But it didn't matter. He knew. It was Thalia's. He'd seen her carrying it around school a million times.

He walked to the nearest safe spot, took a deep breath, and unzipped the bag. He pulled out a map (of New Orleans), three candy bars, a jump rope, a rubber ducky, and a business card that read, *Madame La Rue, Hex Removal. 120 Old Chartres Street, New Orleans.*

Could that be the Muses' next destination? New Orleans? It was far from a sure thing, but it was all he had to go on.

There was one more thing. A small spiral notebook.

Now, it was one thing to look inside a person's bag to see whose it was or to try and figure out where they were off to next. But it seemed quite another to open up Thalia's very own notebook that could be filled with her innermost personal thoughts. Apollo just couldn't do that. He respected Thalia as much as he loved her. He held it for an extra moment, then held it close for a second and started to put it back into the bag. Only he noticed something on the back.

It was a chart.

It was titled "Dylan vs. Apollo."

Under the Dylan side it read,

Pros	Cons
Really funny	*Klutzy*
Happy-go-lucky	*Mortal*
Supercute	*In Denver*

Under the Apollo side it read,

Pros	Cons
A babe	*Hates me*
Romantic	*Domineering*
Smart, charming,	*Controlling*
funny, and brave	*Is in Olympus*

This confirmed his suspicions—Thalia did *not* know he and Dylan were the same person. And the woman who had smacked her gum and kissed him hard with sour breath, the woman who promised to marry him, was *not* his beloved. It only made him more determined. He had to get to Thalia no matter what. He grabbed the bag and the notebook and ran, ran as fast as he could, to the car, jumped in, and tore off like a bat out of Hades.

SIXTEEN

Thursday, 5:16 P.M., Interstate 40, Pocky's mom's car

"We've got to go back!" I cried.

"We're not going back. We've been driving forever already, and even if we did, you'd never find it—you don't even know where you lost it!" yelled Pocky.

"But it had your Madame La Rue business card in it!" I tried appealing to Pocky's immediate needs.

"You know, after what that old woman said, I thought something like this might happen. So I memorized the address just in case. I don't need the card."

"But it has the directions to New Orleans," I said in sheer desperation.

It was my favorite backpack. It was lucky. It had my notebook and my ducky.

"We have a map, and we can get specific directions

when we get to town. We're not going back, Thalia." Pocky was getting more and more assertive as the hex gained power. "And stop pouting," he yelled.

I wasn't pouting. I was merely exercising my right to portray a disdainful grimace on my face in protest of my unfair treatment!

"I need to pee," squealed Era. She couldn't stop squirming in the backseat. With Pocky at the wheel, we were back to driving like regular people—as in, no magic. And it took ages to get anywhere.

"You just went at that diner back there, didn't you?" asked Pocky, terribly impatient with the rest of us.

"Well, yes, but I had two Cokes, and what do you expect? I'm a petite girl."

"We can't stop—we don't have time. We shouldn't even have stopped at that diner," chastised Pocky.

"You got some more turkey and gravy," said Polly, full of sweet, sweet guilt.

"We had to stop, we had to eat, Pock," I said. "It's not like we can magically conjure up food."

Polly looked up from the map and shot me her patented death look from the front seat. She'd forbidden me to use my powers. Again. At all. The rest of this trip. It wasn't exactly fair. I mean, I understood. And I did feel horrible, leading Pocky to believe that Thanksgiving was over when in fact it was really today. And then, well, a lot of people had seemed real upset over the balloon incident. But so far everyone on this trip had gotten to choose a destination except for me, and now we were headed in the opposite direction of one Dylan from Denver. If I could have just used my powers, we could have been in New Orleans like that, gotten this silly hex removed, and in an instant been in Colorado before Dylan, atop some snowy mountain, lost his will to love forever.

Maybe I was being dramatic, but c'mon, the writing was on the wall.

"Hey, we're not too far from Graceland. Let's make a little detour and tour Elvis's mansion!" suggested Polly.

"No! You already picked a place—you can't pick twice!" I cried.

"But Thalia, we're so very close. And it's *Elvis*!"

"No way. I haven't even gotten a pick yet."

"Fine," said Polly through gritted teeth. She appeared to be losing it.

"Fine," I said.

"Thalia, why don't you just pick Graceland? Polly's cranky and . . ." said Era.

"I'm not cranky. And I do not need you to stick up for me, Era, I can take care of myself," yelled Polly.

"You're yelling at me now?" Era was clearly annoyed. "Anyway, I still need to pee. And my butt's all cramped . . ."

"Shush!" Polly yelled at her.

"Don't tell her to shush," I yelled back.

"QUIET!" screamed Pocky at the top of his lungs. "Everyone stop arguing. In fact, unless you have a hex on you, no one is allowed to utter another word!"

We all shut up and rode the rest of the way in silence.

SEVENTEEN

Friday, 11:12 A.M., New Orleans

The drive was slow and boring until we got to the outskirts of New Orleans. There we wove through endless swamps where the air felt sticky and thick and the water looked as still as glass. I wanted to apologize to Polly for being so grouchy earlier, but I couldn't seem to do it. So I just turned my attention to the oncoming lights of the city.

At first sight New Orleans reminded me of New York—tall buildings and lots of lights. But as we got closer, I could see how different it really was. There were lots of smaller houses here, and each house looked more colorful than the next. Most of the streets were lined with these huge trees that seemed to drip thick green leaves like a canopy over our heads. And everything—from the buildings to the street signs to the people—looked old. Not, like, Athens old, but still, older than anything we'd seen in the modern world.

Right before lunchtime we pulled up onto narrow Chartres Street to the house of Madame La Rue. The building had thick moss dripping from every angle and dried skulls in the windows. The porch creaked so loudly, it scared us, and all four of us jumped in unison. Pocky then pulled at the screen door, and it slowly and painfully squeaked open.

"What do you want?" A woman's voice came from the dim hallway. It was evil and dark like molasses. She emerged into the light—her face looked evil, too. She was wearing a turban, and her lips and wrinkly cheeks were smeared with thick makeup.

"I'm looking for Madame La Rue," said Pocky meekly. He sounded exhausted. While we had nodded off in the car, Pocky hadn't slept in over twenty-four hours.

"I am she. Now, what do you want?" If it was at all possible, her voice became more evil.

"Um, your sister sent me, from New York, to get my hex removed. Please, you must help me," said Pocky.

"I am booked solid—I have a very hard case right now. A selfish young girl broke her true love's heart, and now she has a humongous hex on her. It's taking all my energy to remove this one. Come back tomorrow." Was it my imagination, or was she looking pointedly at me?

"No, please!" begged Pocky. "Mine surely can't take too long, please."

"Let me see. Come closer, young man." Madame La Rue's fingers emerged from the extra-long sleeves of her bright purple cloak to pry open Pocky's left eye. She got close to him and peered into his eye from only an inch or two away. I suspected she smelled.

"All right, I can remove your hex today, but you can't leave New Orleans for twenty-four hours. The magic of the city must settle on your skin. If you leave, your hex will only return, I dunno when or where, but it t'will!" She sounded like someone I knew. Someone back home. Maybe that wretched Medusa.* But I'm sure all mean people have a similar quality about them. Like an evil soul sound.

"Twenty-four hours, huh?" said Pocky. Madame La Rue motioned us to wait and disappeared into the back room.

Twenty-four hours? That was it. I was done for. If we stayed here in New Orleans till Saturday afternoon, there was no way that I could get from here to Denver and back to Athens by Sunday.

But if I said something, anything, in the face of poor Pocky's hex, I would truly be the most selfish girl in the world and I wouldn't even deserve to go

---

* A seriously evil girl with snakes for hair and eyes that can turn you into stone.

back home to Olympus. I wanted to see Dylan, I needed to see him, but . . .

"Um, I don't think we can stay here for twenty-four hours. Tomorrow is Sunday, and I have to be back in Athens to pick up my parents." Pocky was almost shaking.

I saw my opportunity to get out of at least one lie, and I went for it. "Pocky, tomorrow's not Saturday—it's only Friday."

Pocky's eyes grew wide, and he looked at Polly and Era. Polly said, "That's right, it's Friday." And then Era nodded.

"Oh, man, that hex must've done a number on my head. I was sure it was Saturday. I mean, Thanksgiving was days ago, wasn't it?"

"No, no, it was yesterday. Are you okay, Pocky?" I said.

"Thank heavens Madame La Rue is gonna lift the hex. I think I'm going crazy." Pocky tapped his forehead for emphasis. "So that settles it—we'll stay here for the next twenty-four hours. Anyway"—he sighed—"I've always wanted to see New Orleans."

"Um, not to be selfish or anything, but I never got to pick a destination," I said quietly. I knew it was no use, but I had to say something. I couldn't help myself.

"Oh, man, Thalia, I feel awful," said Pocky. "I know this hex removal put a little wrench in our

plans. But hey, since it's only Friday, we could probably fit one more place in on our way back to Athens.
Think about where you want to go."

Quietly, sheepishly, I suggested Denver, Colorado.
And then Pocky laughed. He actually laughed.
But then he stopped when he saw the look on my
face. "Thalia! I feel bad and all, but that's only in the
total opposite direction. It's like a gazillion miles
away. It's impossible."

Polly was standing beside Pocky, and I noticed she
had that look on her face. The one she has when the
wheels in her head are turning—when she's figuring
something out. Then her mouth dropped open.
Oops. "That's what this is about?" she sputtered. "It
is, isn't it? Of course, the lying, the mag—" But she
stopped herself. Pocky looked on, confused, but at
that moment Madame La Rue called him into her
back room.

Polly moved in closer to me and seized my arm.
She lowered her voice. "How could you? Have you
not learned a thing? And how did I not see that all
this time you've been trying to lead us on a one-
Muse mission to Denver? We'll never get back to
Olympus—you do realize that, right? Never!" Era's
look of confusion was slowly turning into one of
understanding. Polly stomped off to the opposite
side of the hall in disgust. And then . . . and then
she just dropped her face into her hands and

silently began to cry. I could hear her sniffling through her fingers. Era followed and patted her back sympathetically.

"Polly, I . . ." I said quietly, but Era just looked at me and shook her head. I sat down on the beanbag by the door, feeling utterly, utterly awful.

This place was smelly, like old perfume, like perfume that had been around for a million years. And it was dark and dank and dusty, kind of like what you'd expect Hades to be like. There were jars of crusty bits in every corner, and old apples hung from the ceiling. I hated it here.

I sank back in the beanbag and thought about what I'd done and Denver and Dylan and how I'd used magic when Polly had begged me over and over not to. Selfish, selfish, selfish.

I felt lower than low. And I had to admit, it was looking like fate had no intention of bringing me and Dylan together. Maybe . . . maybe it was time to just admit that it was not meant to be. I wished I had my Apollo vs. Dylan chart so I could add to it. *Dylan— seriously unattainable and not in fate's mind's eye.* That's a con if ever I saw one.

It was time for me to make a choice.

"I am hereby giving up all attempts to get to Dylan and Denver," I said aloud. Guilty as I felt about Dylan, I felt just as guilty about Polly, and I had to do the right thing. Dylan would get over this heartache. I'm cute, but I'm not devastating. The boy would get over me eventually. I hoped.

Polly and Era turned to look at me. I looked at my sneakers. "I have done nothing on this trip but lie and use my powers to turn it into my own little mission to Denver—you're right." I cleared my throat. "I'm not proud of myself. And I'm sorry."

I just fiddled with my laces until a second pair of shoes appeared beside mine. Era plopped down on the beanbag and put her arm around me. Polly just sniffed, and stood, and sniffed again. Then she said, "You know, Thalia, I may be bossy sometimes, but I'm certainly not a monster. If you'd told me you needed to get to Denver, I would have helped you get there."

I didn't know what to say. I'd been too busy going out of my way to prove I wasn't selfish to even ask.

"I'm sorry, Polly."

Maybe she could tell I really meant it. Or maybe the look on my face was just too pitiful for her to bear. Because Polly stopped sniffling and wiped at her eyes with the hem of her sleeve.

"The hex has left the building," hollered Pocky, coming out from behind the curtain, startling all three of us out of our silence. "Well, maybe not yet, but in twenty-four hours it will. Now let's go check into some fine bayou hotel—my treat this time and I'm not taking no for an answer. I say let's take an afternoon catnap, then hit the town, see the sights, and let the magic fall where it may!"

Polly walked over and loomed above me. Then, with a tiny, forgiving smile, she pulled both me and Era up from our chair. I gave her a quick hug and Era, too. I made an inward promise to start thinking, really thinking, about my sisters' feelings before just going with my own wishes. I made another inward promise to get over Dylan from Denver. Then we followed Pocky out the door and into the hot New Orleans air.

EIGHTEEN

Saturday, 10:15 A.M., Café Du Monde, New Orleans

"Oh, these, what are they again, Pocky, they are so yummy!" asked Era.

"They're beignets. Ben-yays! Or really, they're just sugary doughnuts, and they are, as you say, Era, very yummy." Pocky's face was covered in powdered sugar. Era had it in her hair.

"They are so yummy, and I am feeling so good now that my hex is gone, I think I might just need to sing a song," said Pocky. Pocky was known all over Athens for his cute little raps of love.

"Boom sh bop, boom boom sh bop,
Three beautiful chicks and delicious beignets,
You girls are cooler than even Rutherford B. Hayes.
Your beauty with the backdrop of the Mississippi River

Is enough to make a man like me shiver and a quiver.
Life is so good, my hex is no more,
What say you girls and I hit the streets and explore . . .
Boom sh bop, boom boom sh bop."

We gave Pocky a rousing standing ovation. I'd say it was his best song yet. But maybe that's just because it finally wasn't a song in which he professed his love to either me or my sisters.

We were sitting in perhaps my favorite place in New Orleans yet, Café Du Monde. It was just a bunch of cute tables under a big canopy, and they bring you coffee with tons of milk and these yummy beignets! It was crowded with people talking and reading, and there was a guy in the corner playing his saxophone and horse chariots clip-clopping by and it was wonderful. I could have stayed all day.

"I want to go to the Jean Lafitte National Park today," said Polly. She read from the brochure, "'Deep in the heart of New Orleans you'll find a genuine bayou swamp where nature is plentiful and alligators roam free.' Let's go!"

"Seriously, Pol, I am so tired. Let's stay here awhile longer, order another round of the beignets, and then take another New Orleans-style catnap!" I said with all the enthusiasm I could muster. "I mean, I'm tired. We were out late last night, what with those three jazz clubs and the dancing at the Funky

Butt and then that yummy midnight dinner at the Bluebird. Um, I'm pooped."

"No, I want to see the alligators and the swamp boats and hear the Cajun men talk funny. You know what"—Polly shrugged—"I'll go without you. I'll take one of those . . . those . . . those . . . horse carriages!"

"Wait, Polly, I want to go to the"—and this part Pocky said in a fake French accent—"Jean Lafitte Nacional Parke with zee alligators."

"Me too," said Era.

"Fine," I said. A few minutes later they bid me adieu. I sat under the canopy, ordered another three beignets, and kicked back, listening to the sweet sounds of the sax.

✳ ✳ ✳

At Café Du Monde, we sat near the Muses,
These girls never seem to catch on to our ruses.
We heard them make small talk and lay down the facts
That they're going to stay here in New Orleans and relax.
There's been no talk of Denver, no, not for hours,
No question of using any more of their powers.
No worries for us, though, the damage is done,
So let's go to the park and stir up some fun!

✳ ✳ ✳

"This is the coolest," Pocky whispered, his steps slowing down as the group got closer to the swampy area of the Jean Lafitte National Park. Polly and Era had to agree.

The park was exactly what the brochure said: it was wet and dark and a bit creepy. The alligators weren't penned in, but they didn't seem to be a threat, either. They just slept peacefully under a layer or three of thick green muck. You could occasionally see an eye popping out above the slime or maybe a row of scales, but that was all. Still, it was creepy.

The trees were nothing like anything the Muses had seen back home. They were tangled and knotted beyond recognition and covered with a slimy black fuzz. There were surely creatures living in them, but what they were was anybody's guess.

Era, Pocky, and Polly crossed over a wooden bridge that connected one part of the park to the other. While they weren't eager to admit it, they were frightened, and so as they crossed, they clutched one another's hands. Still, at the bottom of the bridge Polly felt the need to talk to one of the gators. She might be a little scared, but she thought they looked so lonely. She leaned over the railing to make eye contact with a peeking reptile. And at that moment a chill, an evil chill, ran across the back of her neck. Distant, girlish laughter echoed across the swamp.

"Polly, be . . ." Era began to pull Polly back from the railing.

Just as she did, a strange, terrifying thing happened. All the alligators began to stir. Slowly at first, then more quickly, every alligator in the swamp began to rise up out of the water and move toward land. And in case you've never seen an alligator move, they get around pretty darn quickly.

Pocky screamed. Polly screamed. Era screamed. They all screamed. And they weren't the only ones. The whole park became overpowered with yelling—a few tourists went running back toward the entrance, waving their cameras and walking sticks like weapons. Pocky sprinted across the bridge, then shimmied up one of the fuzzy trees in terror, an alligator snapping just inches from his ankles.

Polly panicked. She backed herself up against the railing of the bridge, a gigantic gator inching closer and closer to her. "Help! Era! Pocky! Heeeeelp!"

Era had crawled up onto the opposite railing of the bridge, and now she hissed to Polly, very quietly so as not to anger the gators, "Pol? Polly, we have to use magic."

"But—" Polly began to argue.

"No buts. We have to." Amazingly, she was speaking slowly and calmly. "So, on the count of three let's recite the petra personality spell together, okay?"

"Yes, you are right, yes, sure, yes, on three," said

Polly, who was perhaps more scared than ever before in her life.

Era counted off, "One, two, three." Then, "Skylos prosopikotita apodosi," said Era.

"Alligatorus prosopikotita apodosi," said Polly.

A few seconds went by that seemed to last forever. And then, just like that, the alligators, every last one of them, stopped their snapping.

Thank goddess! Polly and Era breathed a sigh of relief. Pocky, having no idea what was going on, stayed in his tree.

The alligators calmed down completely, but they didn't return to the water, either. In fact, the one closest to Polly began rubbing against her leg. The one nearest to Era scratched itself behind the ear, or rather, where its ear would be if alligators had ears.

Several alligators waddled away only to pick up sticks in their jaws and return them to the people they had originally been scaring.

And then the alligator that had been chomping at the bit to have a bite of Pocky's ankle actually, maybe, barked. And then it panted, its tongue just hanging out of its mouth, off to the side. It looked like it was smiling.

"We did it!" cried Era, proud of herself.

"Yes, we did it," Polly agreed. But she did notice the odd behavior of the alligators. "Hey, Era, did I hear you say *skylos* in your chant?"

"I don't think so. But maybe. I might've."

"'Cause you know, the chant is, 'Alligatorus prosopikotita apodosi,'" said Polly.

"Yeah, I know. Um, that's what I said." But Era didn't seem too sure.

"'Cause you know, *skylos* is 'dog,' right, not 'alligator'?"

"Yeah, I know. I'm pretty sure I said *alligatorus*. I think."

"Hmmm, well, it can't hurt to leave them the way they are, right?" said Polly. "I mean, we should do as little magic as possible. And they seem so much more interesting this way. Before, all you got to do was see an eye or two—now you can really interact with the gators." Polly picked up a stick and tossed it into a bush. A pack of alligators leapt clumsily after it.

"Exactly. See, we did good!" cried Era with pride.

"Pocky, get down—that alligator won't hurt you," hollered Polly. "I think we should get back to the hotel, pick up Thalia, and get on our way."

"But it wants my leg," said Pocky, still terribly scared and probably emotionally scarred for life.

"No, it just wants to smell your pants and lick your face, so get down from there. Now!"

And Pocky, none the wiser, slowly climbed down from the tree.

NINETEEN

Saturday, 6:18 P.M., 120 Old Chartres Street,
Ye Olde Po' Boy Shop, New Orleans

Apollo had gotten stuck in Winchester, Virginia, on his way to New Orleans when the car broke down. Apparently he'd been driving with the emergency brake on the whole way, and now the mechanic had to wait for a particular nut and a specific bolt to be delivered on Saturday morning in order to get the car running again.

So when Apollo finally arrived in New Orleans, at the address on the card, and saw not a hex removal service but an Olde Po' Boy sandwich stand, he almost threw in the towel. He went up to the counter and asked the man in the white paper hat if there was a hex removal service on this street or if he'd heard of Madame La Rue or if he'd seen three beautiful girls and a geeky spiky-haired boy, but the man in the white paper hat answered no to all three. Apollo ordered an oyster po' boy with extra-hot sauce (it was a long drive, with no stops) and sat on the curb in frustration, food in hand.

Just as he was taking his first bite of the steaming fried oysters drenched in sauce, a pack of dogs came running up the street toward him. They looked innocent enough, one even had a pink bow in its white poofy hair, but as they got closer, Apollo noticed they were crazed, snapping at everything in sight. He'd seen lots of dogs in his time, even had a pet dog as a young god when he'd brought one back from Athens. But he'd never seen a more ill-tempered-looking pack of canines in his life.

People nearby started running for their lives as the dogs approached, biting and barking, but Apollo stayed on the curb and chewed that first bite. He might not have his magic, but he was a powerful god. He just waited for the dogs to spot him—a seemingly easy target with a yummy sandwich in his hands—and then he stared them—all five of them—down. He looked them straight in the eye, and they stopped dead in their tracks. Then they sort of slunk away, slowly and deliberately.

He watched another man try to approach the same dogs. He was smiling and kneeling and whistling for them to come closer. He even called one of them by name. Apollo just watched with curiosity. The dogs were walking fast but low to the ground, and when they got close to the man, they started snapping their jaws and thrashing their tails. The man turned and started running, and the dogs, led by the one with the pink bow, followed him with wild abandon.

Apollo was beginning to get a strong sense of déjà vu. Those weren't naturally wild dogs. The man had even called one of them by name. Could this possibly be the work of his beloved *again*? With that thought, he found his appetite had vanished.

Apollo stood up, brushed himself off, and threw out the rest of his sandwich. He ran down a quick mental list of possibilities and came up blank. He had no leads, no clues, no nothing. And he felt he had no choice. He hoped the girls were on their way home by now. He would just have to head back, too, and get there before they did. Something told him it was his last chance to warn them about Hera's plans, their questionable future, and the consequences of their actions.

TWENTY

Everyone except Pocky slept in the car on the way home. Sitting in the backseat, I thought about Dylan and I had a good cry. It just made me feel better. And feeling better gave me a new perspective. I saw the bigger issue. My home. My real home, in Olympus. Where, sure, it can be a little boring (especially compared to this trip!), but the rest of my sisters are there and the birds sing the sweetest songs and the food is really delicious. And I had a lot of opportunity waiting for me there. I could bring back all that I'd learned here on this trip and maybe travel throughout Greece or join Athena in a battle or two and maybe even make up with Apollo.

Don't get me wrong—I was still rather upset that

we'd never made it to Denver. But my grief was offset by the knowledge that I'd learned a thing or two about being selfless. And anyway, I'd figure out how to get in touch with Dylan. Somehow. *Without* magic.

Pocky's car pulled up to our house in Athens late Sunday morning. There was plenty of time for him to get to the airport to pick up his parents, plenty of time for us to kick back and contemplate what we'd accomplished on this crazy trip.

We all climbed out of the car with our bags (although I still had one less) and waved good-bye to Pocky. "Hey, girls, thanks for the awesome time!" he yelled.

"Awesome time?" we all said in unison. I found it hard to believe that poor Pocky—what with thinking he'd missed turkey day, getting hexed, and then being chased by alligators—had had an awesome time.

"I love an adventure!" he yelled as he pulled away.

We stood there in the driveway for a moment, staring at the house. It just seemed like ages since we'd been here last, but it was really only four days ago.

"So we made it back to Athens in time for school," said Polly.

"And have I mentioned, dear sister, how much less bossy you seemed on this trip? And how well you stuck up for yourself and your convictions?" said Era to Polly.

"Well, you weren't so bad yourself. You should have seen her at the park, Thalia—she took command, she turned those alligators into docile dogs, she did!"

"So I heard," I said. "And really you seem every day to be more strong and independent, Era."

"I do, don't I?" said Era, totally delighted.

"And me," I said, "I was wholly unselfish."

"Well, not wholly," said Polly. Era kinda shrugged.

"C'mon, I was pretty good, right, in the end. I mean, hello? We never did make it to Denver."

"Well, you did everything you could to try and get there," said Polly.

"Not really. I could've continued to use magic, I could've blinked Pocky into submission and hijacked the car to Denver, but I did no such thing. I think that was incredibly and unfathomably unselfish."

"Yes, yes, that was," said Polly in her most patronizing tone.

I knew I wasn't totally *selfish*. And I knew Daddy would know it soon, too. I just felt it. Era must've felt it, too, because as we walked up the steps to our Athens home, she said, "We'll be home soon."

Polly opened the creaky screen door and then the front door, and then suddenly she dropped her bags

and gasped. Loudly. We took one step inside and followed suit. Even Era screamed.

The room was filled with an eerie green smoke
that smelled of rotten bananas. The lights were
glowing with an unearthly, sickening green glow.
And in the middle of it all, seated on our over-
stuffed floral comfy chair like a green-bellied osisi-
phys waiting to pounce on her prey, was the
abominable, the dastardly, the unthinkable . . . Hera
the evil.

Her face was the color of ripe, peeled beets, an
extreme shade of red, and her nails, we could all see,
were digging into our big floral comfy chair at least
two inches deep. Her ears were twitching ever so
slightly due to the immense amount of steam that
was pouring out of them. And her forest green velvet
dress just oozed over the sides of the chair, hiding
any notion of a real goddess body under there. It gave
the illusion that she was just a giant floating angry
evil head.

"Hera, how lovely to see you. To what do we owe
this honor?" choked Polly in her sweetest tones, as if
she were actually singing the words instead of saying
them.

"Yes, it's rather lovely to see you again—it's been
so long, so very long," added Era. She was now on
half-bended knee and shaking.

I wasn't interested in playing nice. I knew it wasn't

to our benefit, but I couldn't understand why the heck Hera was here, so I had to ask (as rudely as possible), "So, Hera, what brings you?"

The steam continued. The smoke grew even thicker. She cleared her throat like a monster getting ready to dive into dinner and said, "I'm not interested in your niceties, girls, nor, Thalia, your rudeness, any longer. You see, you have disobeyed my rules for the very last time."

"Excuse me, Your Highness, but I don't believe we have," said Era, portraying some of her newfound strength. "For we've in fact accomplished our three goals. I have been far more assertive and independent, Polly has not gotten into anyone's business or been roped into any schemes against her better judgment, and Thalia has been selfless to a fault."

Well, maybe not to a fault, I thought.

"Silence." Hera spoke slowly, deliberately, evilly. "I don't care about such frivolities—those were your father's rules. I'm talking about *my* rules."

You know that feeling, that ill feeling like there is a giant weight in your stomach? The one you get when you've been caught doing something bad and you know you are about to get in a whole lot of trouble for it, but you don't know what kind yet? Take that and multiply it times a hundred and you'll get how I felt at that exact moment.

Hera continued. "I said no magic! And there has been episode upon episode where you have used your magic and wreaked havoc on the mortal world."

Polly cleared her throat. "We really didn't use much at all, and I don't think, with all due respect, Your Highness, that we caused any mortal any real distress," she argued, her voice cracking on the last word.

"Silence!" Hera yelled. "You don't think?" Then she started to laugh her horrible laugh. She pointed her finger, her most powerful finger, her fourth one on her right hand, into the air, and with that the Furies appeared in midcackle. And before our very eyes, before we had time to say anything at all, Alek shape-shifted into the fortune-teller and Tizzie became Madame La Rue. We stood there in horror. Then all three of them morphed into the band the Beautiful Omen, and then in an instant they became those wretched colonial girls. All the while they laughed their torturous laugh. I could hear my own fast-paced breathing; it sounded like a pained echo. The Furies then turned back into themselves, their nasty, wretched selves.

I looked at Polly, who looked at Era, who looked back at me. There was no place to run, not that that would do any good. The Furies grinned from ear to ear as the television buzzed on. I felt my kidneys around my knees. We all turned to watch.

The news was on. Certainly not my favorite show. They were giving a report on New York City, on how the whole darn city was up in arms over the disappearance, into thin air, of their beloved Thanksgiving Day Parade balloons.

Hera laughed some more. The Furies cackled, too.

The Furies swung their heads back in perfect unison as the channel popped to another news program. This one was about New Orleans. "The National Guard has been brought into this affair, and the governor of Louisiana has declared a state of emergency. No one can explain the mystery surrounding the dog problem in the city of New Orleans. It appears that the dogs are destroying this three-hundred-year-old city one bite at a time. Meanwhile, adding to the chaos, the alligators of the surrounding swamps have taken to the streets in search of owners, the comfort of cushy beds, and a nice bowl of dog food."

I looked at Polly and Era. They were both shaking their heads. Their bodies had lost all life—they seemed to be just skin and bones.

"And I should let you know," said Hera, "that the ballroom at Colonial Williamsburg is still undergoing extensive sanitization. Ewww, what a mess." She shivered, and the whole house shook from the foundation up, tossing us three into one another while the Furies just stood there steadfast, their hands on their hips, sick smiles on their faces.

"Zeus, of course, has been defending you, but I'm afraid, well, no, I'm delighted (and with these words she giggled, actually giggled) to tell you that in this matter, ultimately I, the supreme mistress of the god world, have control. There is nothing your daddy can do for you any longer."

The Furies joined hands and began to surround us. I looked over at Era, who looked petrified. I looked over at Polly, who looked devastated. In the face of all that emotion, I was just consumed with guilt. It was most certainly I who had used magic first and, well, the most. All because I wanted to see Dylan, and in the end what had it gotten me? Certainly not Dylan. It had only gotten me fear and guilt and now my horrible, hideous stepmother sitting in my temporary living room, delighted to do . . . what, exactly? I didn't know.

"Hera, you obviously know all about our road trip from Alek, Tizzie, and Meg," I said, "so you must know that it was I who did most, no, all of the magic meddling. I stand here before you and plead with you to spare my sisters the same punishment you have in store for me." I swallowed, afraid of what I was about to do. "Do what you will—banish me to earth forever. But they have been no part of this—"

"Silence!" She laughed again, and this time it made my very own knees shake uncontrollably. "That was very sweet, Thalia, but it will do you no good. And as for this eternal banishment to earth you think you have coming, well, don't you know me by now? I wouldn't be so kind."

The three of us looked at one another with terror in our eyes. Polly and Era both managed to send a small sisterly smile my way underneath all the fright. The Furies closed in on us tighter and tighter.

Hera rose out of the chair and bellowed, "You, dear girls, are hereby banished, all right. You are hereby banished to spend the rest of eternity as servants and slaves to the honorable Blessed Ones, yes, the lovely, fair Furies, in the craggiest pits of the fiery hot, deeply dark, eternally evil . . ."

And then she said the word we were all thinking. The last word we wanted to hear her say. The only word that could take away all hope of ever seeing home or Apollo ever again.

". . . HADES!"

And with that, everything went black.

TWENTY-ONE

Sunday, 12:17 P.M., Athens, Georgia

Apollo dropped off Claire's grandpa's car in silence and slipped the keys into her mailbox without a word. He decided he'd walk from Claire's to Thalia's on foot.

Just a block from Claire's he spotted Pocky driving home, his giant mohawk blowing in the wind. That meant the girls were already back. The nervousness, the fear, the sheer pleasure and joy that were rising up in him from his toes to his head was enough to make him dizzy.

Apollo reminded himself he had to stay on track. He had so much to tell the Muses, but especially Thalia. He needed to tell them about the Furies and warn them against using their powers and tell them about the very real threat of Hera and

Hades that was truly looming over their heads.

He couldn't wait to tell Thalia that he was in fact Dylan and he was sorry he'd deceived her but he was not allowed to reveal himself and how he loved her with all his true heart and knew that she loved him but needed more time and how he just wanted to continue to be her best friend and see where it took them. He longed to talk to her at length about his most recent adventures, and he was dying to hear about hers, for he knew they were extreme. He had seen the trail that Thalia had left behind.

And most important, he thought he'd figured out a way to get the Muses back home, safe and sound in Olympus, before Hera had a chance to strike.

Apollo walked up to the house and took a deep breath and closed his eyes. He couldn't stop the smile, the huge bright smile, from creeping across his face. He could almost taste the moment when Thalia would find out who he really was and take him in her arms. Apollo knocked firmly but coolly.

Nothing.

He knocked a little harder and still nothing.

The door wasn't locked.

Apollo decided to go inside. Strangely, the girls' bags were the first things he saw. They were lying right in the middle of the doorway. Stepping farther in, he noticed that all the lights were on. Everything else looked rather untouched. He called out, "Thalia." Nothing. Then the others. "Era, Polly!" Still nothing. He ran through all the rooms and even peeked outside, up into the old oak tree. Nothing. He went back inside, the smile now gone from his face.

And then he saw it. The huge sunken dent in the big floral chair in the living room. And the burn marks that completely encircled the chair. How could he have missed that when he came in? Apollo began to shake and shiver.

He knew what this meant. It could mean only one thing.

Hera had been here.

He was too late.

The girls were gone . . . for good.

IF YOU THOUGHT THIS
BOOK WAS GOOD, TAKE
A SNEAK PEEK AT
GODDESSES 4,
LOVE OR FATE

The boat finally docked in an overgrown cavern. It was dark, and I smelled the faint scent of cheese. Yes, cheese. That smelly old kind that gets all blue. Only it was like there were mounds of it nearby. It was that smelly.

Charon motioned ominously for us to get out of the boat.

"Where are we supposed to go?" I asked, trying to sound less scared than I was.

He just moved his head slowly toward this eerie light at the other end of the cavern.

"Yes, but where is . . ." and I moved *my* head in the same direction. I know light is supposed to make you feel hopeful and warm, but this light was just plain creepy. Looking at it made the hairs stand up on the back of my neck.

"Miss Thalia, you ask too many questions. You may leave the boat now."

"Well . . . maybe I don't wanna," I said, putting my hands on my hips. I was not budging from this boat until I got an answer. But before I could have a face-off, Polly was dragging me onto the shore by the hood of my orange sweatshirt.

"Enough lollygagging," she said. "Let's get on with this."

"But what is *this*?" whined Era, already standing on the shore beside Polly and looking about.

"You mean *where* is this," I corrected her. Because even though I had a strong suspicion—in fact, an almost certainty—of where *this* was, I just couldn't accept it 'til we knew for sure.

"We'll find out soon enough," said Polly with a sigh and a tremble. She looked frightfully pale but determined. "We don't have a choice. Come on." She stepped farther into the cavern, still holding on to my sweatshirt. As we walked, I grabbed Era's hand and strained my eyes toward the unknown.

"Getting out of the boat was a bad idea," I said to no one in particular. "A bad, bad idea. Charon will just have to let us get back on. I don't care if we float in that boat forever, as long as . . ." But when I turned back to look at the water, Charon had already floated away—leaving us on the bank of this smelly moaning river in the deep depths of this vile cavern.

Not knowing what else to do, I trudged along behind my sisters. The light ahead got brighter and brighter as we walked, and finally we emerged into a scene I can hardly describe.

The gates were hanging open, apparently awaiting our arrival. They were tall and glistening like black ink, and they were easily eight stories high and made of steel with sharp points sticking all about. There were gruesome gargoyle heads and winged monsters on every post, and the whole gigantic thing was wrapped in oversized metal chains that made a deep noise as they clunked together slowly in the cold, cold wind that was suddenly howling all around us.

We walked through them in awe. In giant letters across the top of one side of the gate, it said . . .

"Tart," I read out loud.

"Tart?" asked Era, her trembling lips spreading into a shaky, hopeful smile. "Well, I do love tarts. . . ."

Clang! Clunk!

The gates closed behind us with an invisible force and a ruckus that made me queasy.

"Oh, Goddess!" Polly said, having turned to take a look. I followed her gaze. The cave we had just emerged from was no longer there—it had disappeared completely into a solid rock wall. The only thing remaining was the closed gates, and even though the words along the top were now backward, we could read them clear as day.

The only one who said it aloud was Era. Said what we all knew but didn't want to know. Said the unthinkable.

"Tart. Arus. Oh."

A small groan escaped Polly's lips. Era's bottom lip stuck out, and her big gray-blue eyes filled with tears. I had to do something to fix this. But what?

"You know, I think we could fit in between those posts over there. Let's make a run for it," I whispered.

"To where? Where shall we run to?" demanded Polly—also in a whisper—her face whiter than Pegasus's snow-white fur.

I didn't answer. I didn't have time. Because at that moment the scariest, beastliest animal I have ever seen came lunging at us out of nowhere! It snarled and it growled and it drooled a green gook and it was immediately towering above us.

"Ahhhhh!" we all screamed in unison, running back against the gate and, seeing that we were at a dead end, hugging each other under the giant U.

The thing, the four-headed monster thing, had four sets of fangs, and each one seemed sharper than the next, and each one was dripping with bubbling slobber. All eight of his eyes were bright red like hot fire pokers, and they were all trained squarely on us.

I clasped tightly to each of my sisters as we cowered against the gate. Era was now at my feet, her eyes squeezed shut. She was gripping my pant leg so fiercely that it was beginning to rip. Dust was swirling around us; the wind was whistling an ugly, off-key tune. Everything got darker. And I couldn't stop shivering. *This can't be our fate, this can't be our fate,* I kept saying to myself over and over again, feeling tears come to my eyes.

Was this it? Was this what I'd led my sisters into, through all my selfishness and my lying? Would we never see Apollo, or our other sisters, or our home ever again?

And as the beast got closer, I had time to ask myself one final question.

Where, oh, where, was Daddy?